EBURY PRESS

CURSE OF THE PIR

Mukesh Singh is an Indian Police Service officer of the Jammu and Kashmir cadre. He is a BTech in civil engineering from the Indian Institute of Technology Delhi. He joined the Indian Police Service in 1996 and has headed several sensitive assignments as district superintendent of police in Reasi, Pulwama, Poonch and Jammu during the peak of terror activities. He was a part of the core team that set up the National Investigation Agency, which is now the premier counterterrorist investigation agency in the country. He served there in the capacity of superintendent of police, deputy inspector general and inspector general. He currently heads the police of Jammu province as the additional director general of police.

During his service, Mukesh has always been at the forefront of counterterror operations, be it in the field in Jammu and Kashmir in various capacities or at the National Investigation Agency, where he investigated some of the most high-profile cases.

He has co-authored a book, *Police Operations*, and has also co-published three papers: 'Investigation of Encounter Killings' (2016); 'Police Operations' (2015) and 'Conducting an Anti-Terrorist Operation' (2014).

Anupama Pandey studied at some of the premier institutes of India and worked in the development, private and government sectors, before stepping down from the position of state nodal officer at Mission Swaraj, Government of National Capital Territory of Delhi, to pursue her passion. A traveller at heart and a person who enjoys both solitude and the company of others, she is a trained relationship coach and life coach, and is the founder of anupamapandey.com. *Curse of the Pir* is her first book.

Celebrating 35 Years of
Penguin Random House India

CURSE
OF THE
PIR

**MUKESH SINGH
ANUPAMA PANDEY**

EBURY
PRESS

An imprint of Penguin Random House

EBURY PRESS

USA | Canada | UK | Ireland | Australia
New Zealand | India | South Africa | China | Singapore

Ebury Press is part of the Penguin Random House group of companies
whose addresses can be found at global.penguinrandomhouse.com

Published by Penguin Random House India Pvt. Ltd
4th Floor, Capital Tower 1, MG Road,
Gurugram 122 002, Haryana, India

Penguin
Random House
India

First published in Ebury Press by Penguin Random House India 2023

Copyright © Mukesh Singh and Anupama Pandey 2023

ISBN 9780143461098

Typeset in Adobe Caslon Pro by MAP Systems, Bengaluru, India
Printed at Thomson Press India Ltd, New Delhi

www.penguin.co.in

To all the personnel of the security forces
who laid down their lives in the fight
against terror outfits to protect their countrymen

Chapter 1

It could well have been a scene straight out of a Bollywood movie. Nikita's mother was busy giving instructions. 'He's a good boy. I'm sure a lot of people are trying to get him for their daughters. We're lucky that the matter has reached this far. Now that he is coming to meet you, make sure that you speak only when spoken to! There is absolutely no need to start a conversation. Just because you are a doctor, you don't have to go about flaunting how smart you are.'

Nikita silently prayed that her mother would stop speaking, and set the example of 'speak only when spoken to'.

Nikita's younger sister, Payal, who was also getting dressed, could sense the rising tension in the room. She broke into the song. '*Mai chali, mai chali, dekho pyaar ke gali, mujhe roke na koi, mai chali mai chali …*'

Nikita smiled. She said, 'Why don't you marry this guy in front of whom you can't even speak when not spoken to,' and glared at her mother.

Sensing that the time had come for her to exit the room and leave her daughters to themselves, Nikita's mother

1

left, pretending she had lots of errands to run before the guests arrived.

Nikita looked into the mirror and was satisfied. She was wearing a simple pink salwar kameez with floral prints on it. The soft pink chiffon dupatta enhanced her fair complexion. If she were being honest with herself, she was keen to meet this Rajveer character, who her family was raving about. She had been told that he was an IPS officer in the Jammu and Kashmir cadre. She had learnt from conversations in the family that he had been a sincere student and had cracked the IIT and then the civil services exams on the first attempt. Who does that? What a mad guy. Did he do nothing but study all his life? How boring! Plus, look at the dim-witted guy—he first studied for IIT, took a seat (killing someone else's chance) and then studied for the civil services. What madness! If only he had asked her, her advice to him would have been to loaf around for three years while doing a non-technical degree, then study for a year and a half like a madcap, and crack the civil services. Maybe he needed her company to think clearly in life. She tapped her finger on her right temple and smiled.

Coming from a family of doctors, Nikita was the bridge between her younger and elder siblings. Her elder brother had studied medicine and was practising with their father in his clinic. They were often found discussing cases even at home and sometimes at the dinner table. While she was growing up, medicine seemed to be a natural option and she pursued the course without much thought to it. As she grew up, she was sure that she did not want to marry a doctor because she did not want to discuss cases at home and certainly not at the dinner table. Rajveer was quite distant from the medical field, which suited Nikita just fine. Payal was the happy-go-lucky kid who kept the madness alive in the otherwise sombre atmosphere of their home. Breaking the family tradition of producing doctors, Payal had chosen to be a fashion designer. She was in college and behaved like she was in school.

***

On the other side of the city, Rajveer was preparing for the meeting too.

Rajveer came from a conservative and humble family. He was the elder of two boys, and his sincerity towards his role as elder brother made his younger sibling always feel well protected. In fact, Rajveer was the type who always kept a close watch on the friends his brother had, the books he read, the places he visited and the way he spent his free time, playing the father figure to the hilt. His homemaker mother was eager to get him married and was looking forward to having another woman for company. His father, a government employee in the Post and Telegraph Department, was the perfect support to his religious and pious mother. When the results of the Union Public Service Commission (UPSC) examination were announced, he was overjoyed and immediately booked tickets for a visit to Mata Vaishno Devi to express his gratitude. The entire colony had celebrated the good news and the line of visitors coming to congratulate Singh sahab added to his joy and pride.

Following in the footsteps of his elder brother, Rajveer's younger brother, Suresh, had also joined IIT and was now working in a public sector undertaking. He, too, was eager for Rajveer to marry because he had a girlfriend and wanted his path cleared before he broached the topic with his parents.

Knowing his brother well, Suresh teased him saying, 'Senior IITian, ready with your set of questions? Interview *ke liye taiyaar?*'

Rajveer gave him a dirty look and said, 'I'm shitting bricks. I wonder what's in store for me. Meeting random girls and making conversation with them is not my cup of tea.'

With a naughty wink, Suresh's repartee came. 'Making love is?' If looks could kill, Suresh would be dead that day!

Neither Nikita nor Rajveer had any fixed idea of the person they wanted to marry. Bollywood had not managed to influence either of them. However, Nikita did want some romance in her life and did wish to be bought gifts on her birthday and anniversary. She would be extra happy if she got gifts for no reason at all. Shopping was not high on her list, but it was still there on the list. Rajveer, on the other hand, wanted an intelligent girl who was grounded enough to take care of his parents and support him when the need arose. Good looks were not really on his list, but he did want to marry a pleasant-looking girl with likeable mannerisms.

Rajveer looked at the photograph in his hand. He liked what he saw. A tall, fair girl with a confident smile was looking straight at him. She exuded self-assurance and a certain level of buoyancy, which made her look much prettier than she actually was. *She looks so different from me. Is that rule—opposites attract—really true*, he asked himself with a smile. His IITian brain was at work once again.

The picture Rajveer had sent was the most uninteresting thing Nikita had seen when it came to matrimonial pictures. It was a passport-size picture; he probably used it while filling in the UPSC form, she thought. How on earth do these guys actually hope to marry? And to marry someone as fun-loving as her?! Then she remembered what her grandmother often said in colloquial Hindi, '*Ghee ka laddoo, thehdo bhla.*' Sweets made in pure ghee are great even though they do not look good.

Nikita glanced at herself in the mirror from the corner of her eyes and told herself, 'Let's meet this *ghee ka laddoo.*'

Chapter 2

Information received from well-planted sources revealed that the commander of the Lashkar-e-Jabbar, Tariq bhai, was resting inside a hideout in the sleepy *kasba* of Heff Shrimal. It was a cold winter morning in January 2014, but this posed no deterrent to the Indian security forces. Once the information was received, preparations were quickly made and the necessary groups were given the go-ahead to scan the area in Shopian district, known to be infested with terrorists. Security forces swooped down on the house where the hideout was. It belonged to a man called Muzammil.

The Special Operations Group (SOG) of the J&K Police got to work and went through Muzammil's house with a fine-tooth comb. S.P. Showkat, popularly known as Apollo, was the district superintendent of police of Shopian. Apollo was a corrupt officer but had made a name for himself because of his capacity for intelligence generation and operational acumen. He had a terrific sense of humour and was much liked by his colleagues and subordinates. Once, when asked why he would fleece transporters plying their vehicles on the national highway, he replied with his trademark sense of humour: 'Sir, when the vehicle enters from Punjab and moves towards the Kashmir Valley, the vehicle owner is stripped by many districts along the national highway. By the time it reaches his district, he is practically naked. How can I fleece him in this condition?'

Apollo had acquired his nickname not only because of his huge build, which made him look like the famous Apollo tyre, but also because he was always dependable as far as counterterror operations were concerned. Now, he couldn't but appreciate the opulence of the house and wondered where all this money was coming from. *Well, Muzammil is certainly a man with expensive tastes,* he thought. The lush carpets on Italian marble flooring, the crystal knobs, the exquisite figurines and showpieces—all spoke volumes about the owner of the house and the pains taken to make it so beautiful.

Though Apollo was impressed by this display of wealth, he was also intrigued as to the source of it. As part of the routine process, Muzammil was summoned. By way of conversation, Muzammil credited the vast apple orchards as the source of his wealth, his magnificent house and his ostentatious lifestyle.

Muzammil did not try and stop the forces from carrying out their search operations and everyone relaxed a bit. The inhabitants and the SOG began to share jokes and laugh together. Yet, while on the surface the atmosphere was easy-going, the search party was very focused, and the inhabitants of the house were still very alert.

Apollo sent his core team to clear the second floor. The search continued as per the prescribed format, and while the men were upstairs, Muzammil shared some anecdotes with Apollo on the first floor. While all this laughing, chatting and search operations were going on simultaneously, a young boy of about fourteen, wearing a pair of blue jeans, grey *phiran* and sports shoes, jumped out from the second-floor window and made his way to the back exit. All the laughter and chatting stopped.

The cordon was tight though, and there was no scope to escape. SOG sub-inspector Athar Mehmood blocked the path of the young lad and brought him down.

The boy, Mohammed Irfan, trembled as he said, *'Janab*, I got scared seeing the security forces and ran out of fear.'

Search operations continued while Mohammed Irfan was taken to 'Baba One', the makeshift joint interrogation centre at Shopian. Baba One was a dreaded interrogation centre in the initial years of terrorism in Jammu and Kashmir; it was where most of the top terrorist commanders were interrogated. Some of them died during interrogation and it was commonly believed that this centre was haunted and one could hear shrieks at night. However, over a period of time, Baba One had fewer visitors and turned into more of a recreation centre where SOG personnel would come and watch TV. The lack of VVIP visitors had turned it into a dilapidated structure.

'Ek do teen ...' On a big LED TV screen, Madhuri Dixit was dancing to the popular tune, and Irfan's attention was immediately captured. The atmosphere of the centre was much more casual than what Irfan had anticipated, and he began to relax.

Irfan was so engrossed in the loud music and the dancing on the screen that he did not notice another person entering the room. The investigation team had invited an Ikhwan leader, Bakshi, to help with the interrogation. He was one of the few surviving Ikhwanis who worked with the SOG. The Ikhwanis had been terrorists before surrendering to the security forces in the mid-1990s, after a large section of them became disillusioned with the policies and actions of the terror groups. At the time of their surrender, they all belonged to the terror outfit Hizbul Mujahideen, controlled and funded by the Pakistani authorities. After their surrender, the men were placed with various SOGs to bring them under some form of command, control and supervision. They turned into a huge force multiplier after their surrender and helped the security forces carry out a number of counterterror operations, being well-versed with the modus operandi, contacts and hideouts of the largest terror outfit in Jammu and Kashmir at that time.

Now, Bakshi took over the interrogation of Irfan. He was a seasoned investigator and began with casual conversation.

Speaking in Kashmiri, he put Irfan at ease by talking about the time of Eid. Bakshi chatted about how he would collect Eidi from the town and Irfan began to open up and shared some of his own Eid stories. Seeing a window of opportunity to prove that he was all grown up and good at his work, he talked about how he, along with three other boys his age, once went from shop to shop, practically extorting a handsome Eidi from each one of them. It gave each of them a sense of satisfaction to know that they were being given responsibilities that the other men would usually handle. As he chatted, he revealed that a local guide, Ashfaq, had brought Tariq bhai and his associates the previous night to his house, and they had stayed the entire night.

Ashfaq had an extremely lazy but surprisingly alert pet dog called Aloo, Irfan said. Aloo lived up to his name not just in colour but also in size. Ashfaq was never alone because Aloo was always with him. That night, Ashfaq, with Aloo beside him, stood outside the house as a lookout. Though Aloo looked like a potato, he was true to his breed and, early the next morning, he started barking at the sound of the footsteps of strangers in the village. Inside the house, the men figured out that a cordon was being laid. Tariq bhai was immediately alerted and, without any further delay, he left with his bodyguard.

'That Mehmood bhai of the nearby kasba was also with Tariq,' Irfan said.

Bakshi pretended to look puzzled as if he was trying to recollect which Mehmood Irfan was talking about: '*Kaun Mehmood bhai?*'

'The one who works as a guide for the mujahids. These days work is less, since winter has set in,' Irfan answered.

Bakshi pointed to the left and said, 'The person who lives in this kasba?'

'*Ji janab.* He lives in Imam Saheb.'

The conversation went on for a few minutes more. When Bakshi realized that there was no more to be got from Irfan, he left to make a call.

Based on the information received from Bakshi, Apollo moved his team towards the neighbouring village, Imam Saheb. Bakshi was very familiar with Imam Saheb as he was from a village nearby and had earlier served as the area commander of Imam Saheb with the Hizbul Mujahideen. He told Apollo to pick up the sarpanch of the village and ask about Mehmood bhai's house. Apollo immediately dispatched a team to pick up the sarpanch, who showed them Mehmood bhai's house.

Mehmood was quickly apprehended and interrogated. Meanwhile, Apollo calculated the distance that Tariq bhai could have travelled on foot in two hours and asked his team to alert all exit points. Immediately complying with orders, road barricades with signages clearly informing vehicles to stop were put up at all the exit points, ensuring that no one could leave without the knowledge of the authorities.

It took very little effort to make Mehmood start speaking. He told the officers that Tariq bhai was probably in the house of a man called Aslam, who resided on the outskirts of Imam Saheb. Mehmood went so far as to offer to take the security forces to Aslam's house, on the condition that he would be let off once they reached.

As a matter of normal procedure, the SOG personnel cordoned off Aslam's house immediately. When the SOG reached there with Mehmood, the guide volunteered to go inside and look for Tariq bhai. Citing his long association as a fellow mujahid and a friend, he said he was confident that he would be able to convince the Lashkar-e-Jabbar commander to surrender. Mehmood's relaxed body language prompted the security forces to let him give it a shot. They waited outside, well entrenched behind safety walls with their weapons pointing towards the cordoned house, covering each exit route from the building.

Soon, Mehmood could be seen at the doorway, a big smile on his face and giving them a thumbs-up sign. It was then that SOG sub-inspector Athar Mehmood, with all his experience in counterterror operations, made the biggest mistake of his life. He let his guard down and began to move towards the house. Almost in a flash, as if everything was happening at 2x speed, the whole operation collapsed. As soon as he entered the compound, rapid firing started. Athar was shot in the head and fell to the floor in a pool of blood. Often, when we think of things that we've done, we look back and can see that it was foolhardy, but in the moment, it seemed the most correct thing to do. Athar had one such moment when he trusted Mehmood and his signal.

His colleagues, hurt more by the shots that had brought down Athar, put in their best effort. They held on to his feet and tried to pull him away while simultaneously firing back at the terrorists. They could see Mehmood and Tariq bhai, holding AK-47 rifles, shooting at them. Finally, the forces decided to retreat, unable to withstand the rapid and random volume of fire from inside the house. The badly battered bulletproof Mahindra Commander vehicle—popularly known as Rakshak—reversed into the compound, driven by one of the SOG commandos. They somehow managed to pull Athar's body into the vehicle and drove away.

The stage was now set for a full-fledged encounter with the terrorists. Tear gas shells were fired to incapacitate the terrorists, but the forces outside were affected at the same time because of the way the wind was blowing. After a four-hour encounter, a mini drone was flown into the house and inside the room on the top floor to assess the situation. Video footage showed two bodies on the floor, lying still; and a third person, barely able to move his hand, but clearly alive. The SOG team immediately stormed the house and cleared the rooms one by one, making sure that no mistake was made this time. The final tally: two terrorists dead and one caught alive in an injured condition.

The injured terrorist was none other than Tariq bhai, the commander of the Lashkar-e-Jabbar, of south Kashmir.

* * *

Tariq bhai's actual name was Manzoor Trali—like most terrorists, he operated under a code name. The title 'Trali' came from the fact that he was a resident of village Tral, a hotbed of terror in the Kashmir Valley primarily because of its proximity to the mountains and dense forests that provided a safe haven for terrorists, and which also could be used as a training ground.

Manzoor Trali was short and had a stocky build. He was often called Pir sahib, meaning messenger of Allah. A self-motivated terrorist, he was convinced that there was no other way to achieve the organization's goal other than violence. Jihad, for him, was fighting Indian security forces against what he called the 'forceful occupation of Kashmiri land'.

Manzoor Trali was taken to the nursing room in Baba One where Dr Dawood, popularly called Dr Dang, attended to him. He had some splinter injuries on his back and a bullet injury in his stomach, which luckily for him had missed all the vital organs. Dr Dang cleaned and bandaged his wounds, and administered a saline drip to infuse some energy into Trali. Dr Dang knew that the SOG personnel did not like to waste time before starting interrogation, and therefore, had his drills set. Unless the patient was so serious that he needed to be shifted to a bigger hospital, the doctor would give his go-ahead for interrogation. As soon as the SOG men got a green signal indicating that Trali was fit to answer questions, the interrogation started.

Interrogating people like Trali could be both challenging and fun at the same time. Trali was an expert in weaving tales and diverting the interrogation into a religious debate. On the other hand, he could be fun as well. On one occasion, he made a tongue-in-cheek comment, and the interrogating officer could not help but smile. In fact, it became a standing joke among the interrogating team. Trali's famous lines were, *'Janab, aap aur mai to besan aur aloo ke tarah hain. Is room ke jalte hue tel me hum dono saath san ke fry hote hain.* (Sir, the two of us are like potato and gram flour. We both get mixed and fried in the same pan of oil.)'

The superintendent of police knew this about Trali and kept the questions pointed and direct. He asked, 'What do you think about terrorists throwing grenades at young couples sitting inside parks?'

Trali replied, 'See when there is a flood, muck and dirt from the sides enter the main flow of water. But over time, as the flood travels a distance, the dirt again separates and goes to the side and what finally flows is clear water.' Jihad, therefore, to him, was like a flood, which initially tended to get some wrong people into the fold. But over a period of sustained struggle, what remained was a struggle free from the bad elements.

The man sounded so convincing, Apollo feared that he might sway the team interrogating him. He asked for the camera to be switched off and ordered his men to leave the room. Manzoor Trali was then treated to interrogation methods including 'tadpad' or flogging with a leather belt attached to a wooden handle, 'cheera' or the 180-degree stretching of legs and waterboarding before Apollo took over the interrogation. It seemed that Trali needed this last push because he began speaking.

'I was one of the first volunteers to join the Lashkar-e-Jabbar after its formation by Maulana Majid Asgar,' he began.

Maulana Majid Asgar was a pir who came to Kashmir via Bangladesh on a valid passport and visa. He was initially a part of the Harkat-ul-Mujahideen—this was in 1993—and had been specially sent to Kashmir to rally and reorganize various groups operating in the Kashmir Valley. Maulana Asgar was a big man, so overweight he could barely move. He had a deep understanding of the holy texts and interpreted them as it suited the mujahideen. He was a great orator, good at religious preaching and extremely convincing. There were plenty of combatants among the mujahideen, but they lacked a maulana who could bind them together by referencing the holy texts.

Maulana Asgar was apprehended during a casual search at a police *naka* near Bijbehara. He was then sent to Kot Bhalwal Jail in Jammu. Kot Bhalwal was specially chosen with a view to keeping him away from the mujahideen, considering his clout among the terrorist groups, and to avoid creating a new centre for terrorists in the jail premises. Maulana Asgar slowly made himself popular inside the jail.

So much so that even some serving government officials would visit the jail to seek *tabeej* (amulet) from him to ward off the evil eye.

Maulana Asgar was important to the Pakistanis. With him in Kot Bhalwal Jail, far away from the battleground, the morale of the mujahideen was low. Three attempts were made to get him released from the prison. In the first attempt, Hafiz Sheikh, a British terrorist of Pakistani origin, abducted three foreign nationals in India in October 1994 and sought the release of the maulana in exchange for them. After a series of police cordon and search operations, in which three policemen were killed, the abducted foreign nationals were released. India held on to the prize possession. In the second attempt, terrorists of Al-Jihad abducted four foreign nationals from Pahalgam in Anantnag district in 1995. Out of four, one was beheaded, one escaped and the fate of the remaining two was still unknown—in all likelihood they were killed. This incident invited heavy international criticism and harmed the mujahideen rather than benefiting them. In the third attempt, in December 1999, an Air-India flight, AI-214, was hijacked and taken to Kandahar. The hijackers, who were relatives and close associates of Maulana Asgar, demanded his release and that of another terrorist, Mastan Sheikh. Taking into account the safety of the passengers, both men were released in Kandahar. Besides the obvious Pakistani support, the release of Maulana Asgar was facilitated by Al-Qaeda and the Taliban, who provided tactical and material support.

After reaching Pakistan, Maulana Asgar started a new organization, which was named Lashkar-e-Jabbar, and pursued his objective of violent jihad in India.

Maulana's plans soon picked up momentum. He started recruiting actively: physically in Pakistan and through a proxy in the Kashmir Valley. Among his initial recruits were Haji Baba, the mastermind behind the Indian Parliament attack, and Manzoor Trali, who trained in Afghanistan, initially near the Bagram Airbase, alongside the Taliban.

Manzoor Trali had joined the organization after listening to the powerful speeches sent by Maulana through audio tapes smuggled across the border with the infiltrating mujahideen. He was arrested in 2004 with an arms consignment in Delhi; the arms were meant for another attack on the scale of the one on the Indian Parliament. He was awarded a life sentence. The Lashkar-e-Jabbar backed this pir with all their might. They paid for his lawyer expenses by wire transfer from Dubai. Even from jail, Trali was capable of building up his cadre. His lawyers negotiated his transfer to Srinagar Jail on health grounds, where he found a ready Lashkar-e-Jabbar cadre waiting for him to join and lead them. When he was entering the high-security Srinagar Jail, the terror associates lodged there gave him a rousing reception, with men from the Hizbul Mujahideen and the Lashkar-e-Jabbar lining up in two flanks to cheer him.

The lawyers then worked harder. They managed to get him released on parole on grounds of 'good behaviour'. The security forces did not know at that time what was going on in the mind of this master jihadi, who was no less than the Maulana in stature in the Kashmir Valley. He went on to lead the Lashkar-e-Jabbar in various attacks and helped receive their infiltrators in and around the Awantipora and Tral areas of Jammu and Kashmir.

'Once,' he said, 'I took a Pakistani terrorist of the Lashkar-e-Jabbar to the local Border Security Force camp and introduced him as my "mureed", follower.' The local BSF commandant treated him well, and hosted the pir and his mureed to a sumptuous lunch, little realizing that while this was going on, the Pakistani mureed was continuously doing a reconnaissance of his camp. The mureed, Abu Maaz, carried out a fidayeen attack—a suicide attack—at the BSF camp a week later.

For Apollo, Trali was a big catch. He made some important disclosures which led to operations in and around south Kashmir. Apollo needed this operation's success to salvage his reputation of being a corrupt officer. In the Kashmir Valley, success in counterterrorism operations was the biggest indicator of a successful officer.

Manzoor Trali was later sent to Srinagar Jail. Apollo maintained contact with him, sending emissaries from time to time to give him some goodies, in return for information.

Chapter 3

'Who do you like more? Shah Rukh or Salman?' Rajveer asked, not knowing where to start the conversation.

Nikita pondered for some time, and then shrugged as she said, 'Neither.'

Actually, deep down, Rajveer just wanted to know Nikita's romantic preferences. His biggest failing, as he saw it, was that he did not see himself as a romantic person at all. In fact, as much as he wanted to be free and natural in the presence of the opposite sex, he found himself even more restricted. Added to this was the fact that a senior whom he was chasing for some notes had once told him, 'If you follow up this much with a woman, you will end up with a love marriage.' This simple and casual snide remark had added to Rajveer's anxiety in front of women. He was now very hesitant to approach them.

Meanwhile, Nikita was thinking, *Why would someone want to know which Bollywood hero I like? Has the world come to this? Do people decide whom to marry based on their choice of Bollywood celebrities?*

At the same moment, Rajveer was thinking how lucky he was that at least one girl in the world did not want her future husband to be like the screen heroes.

After a few awkward moments, the conversation moved on to their favourite dishes, books, music, their friends …

Though the conversation did not quite go the way it does in Bollywood movies, they ended up having a good time together—just twenty minutes, though, because that was the time given to them to decide who they wanted to spend the rest of their lives with!

The innocent and sweet meeting led to an exchange of letters. Rajveer was always very measured in his selection of words—the snide remark from his senior always plaguing him. Nikita, on the other hand, was as vivacious and unabashed when writing as she was while speaking. It would be a good balance.

On 11 May 1999, they got married.

Though she did not have any particular preference, Nikita wanted to go abroad for their honeymoon. Rajveer made arrangements for a holiday in Mauritius, and the couple planned to leave two days after their wedding. Nikita was the envy of her friends and cousins.

But destiny had alternate plans.

The Kargil War broke out on 3 May 1999, and Rajveer's leave was cancelled. He was asked to report to work. Without any hesitation or regret, Rajveer cancelled his honeymoon plans and made an offer to Nikita to either stay behind with his parents for a while or accompany him to J&K. Nikita, initially a little upset about the development, was quick to see the larger picture and responded with conviction and a smile, 'I'll join you. Let's go to J&K. I know it's a beautiful place.'

Rajveer smiled back. He had a friend for life.

Jammu and Kashmir was indeed beautiful. But, in the midst of the Kargil War, three days after their marriage, when they landed in Poonch district, the place looked more frightening than beautiful. Nikita was exposed to the most unusual situations. As a young woman of twenty-six who had traded Mauritius for Poonch, she had expected a quiet home and some peaceful time with her husband of three days. Instead, she was treated to firing near their residence in the Mendhar sub-division.

'The way to a man's heart is through his stomach. Always remember that,' her mother had repeatedly told her and cautioned her not to let house help take over the kitchen completely. As days passed, she tried her best to cook new dishes and her culinary skills actually improved. One evening, she prepared Thai food and waited for Rajveer to get back home. She laid out the table carefully with their new crockery and cutlery. Pleased, she smiled to herself and looked in the mirror. Why not surprise Rajveer? She tried on a new outfit and changed her footwear to match the dress. She put on some make-up too.

Her efforts didn't go to waste. Rajveer was surprised. She looked so lovely, all his tiredness faded. He asked her to let the house help leave early that evening, hoping to spend some private moments with her.

He went over to the music system to put on some light music, but even before he could touch the play button, he heard firing near his house. He rushed to a confused and scared Nikita and pushed her to the ground, where they both lay still. The sentry at the gate retaliated and an exchange of fire continued for some time. To prevent any stray bullet from entering through the window, Rajveer had covered it with his bulletproof jacket.

After about five minutes, the firing stopped and the sentry called out to Rajveer: 'Sir, they have run away.'

This was normal during that period in Mendhar. Terrorists would sneak in at night, fire randomly at the target house and then flee. Once Rajveer got the green signal from the sentry, he helped Nikita get up. Soon, they were in makeshift army bunkers, eating dosa arranged from a nearby home. 'The way to a man's heart is through his stomach. Always remember that,' rang in Nikita's head.

After a couple of weeks, Nikita learnt to expect the unexpected. She waited for Rajveer but was prepared for quick action at short notice. Somewhere inside, she felt she had grown stronger in just a short time.

But what came next was not something she was prepared for; it challenged her and the thought that she was 'prepared to expect the unexpected'.

One morning, a flurry of police and army personnel arrived and began to cover the area around their home. An officer approached her, introduced himself and assured her of her safety. He informed her in measured official tones that there had been an ambush on Rajveer's vehicle while he was returning from a training session. He assured her that Rajveer was safe and would be joining her soon. All the security personnel there would ensure the safety and security of Rajveer's wife and his house.

Nikita put up a brave front. She smiled and said, 'I am sure he is fine. Would you like to have a cup of tea or coffee while we wait for him to get back?' The gentleman officer smiled back, silently appreciative of her poise, and politely refused the offer.

Rajveer eventually came home late in the night, exhausted. After a short but much-needed hot shower, he emerged. He was in a rather sombre mood that day. He was usually a man of few words anyway, but that evening he could safely be called a man of 'fewer' words. He was either lost in his own world or exhausted, but all Nikita got in reply to her questions about what had happened, was a small smile, a nod and a gesture indicating that he had a heavy head and wanted to rest. He collapsed on the bed and was asleep even before one could spell L-O-V-E.

Chapter 4

Love has many dimensions. Some straight and clear. Some very convoluted and twisted. Terrorist entities believe that jihad is a form of love.

Just as the love between Rajveer and Nikita was beginning to blossom and a bond was forming between them, the members of the Lashkar-e-Jabbar were increasing the activities for their jihad. As desire between Rajveer and Nikita rose, terrorist activities in Jammu and Kashmir also reached a peak. As Rajveer and Nikita made every effort to use the time they had to learn more about each other with each passing day, Pakistan pushed all the foreign terrorists present in J&K on a recruitment spree while the Indian Army was busy on the battlefront at Kargil.

In fact, several terrorist organizations were active in Kashmir. Lashkar-e-Taiba was one of them. Lashkar-e-Taiba was not one to trust the local Kashmiris, but in an effort to impress the ISI with its strength in numbers and power in participation, it allowed the entry of local Kashmiri boys into its fold. Several of the discussions

Rajveer and his colleagues had over lunch revolved around the speed at which these recruitments were taking place. It was common for officers to discuss these issues during their break; in fact, these lunch sessions often turned into brainstorming sessions on strategy.

It was through these discussions that Rajveer found out that everything actually revolved around money. The inside story behind this competitiveness between the terrorist outfits was the handsome funding that the ISI handed out to the mujahideen every month. It was all very clear in terms of funding: the organization that had more people and gave the impression of causing maximum damage got the most funding.

That day, Rajveer finished his lunch and, in the privacy of his office, made a short call to Nikita. 'Lunch was very good today. I know you've been cooking these days. Why don't you just get some rest before you return to Delhi and your work and the usual maddening schedule?' Rajveer said.

'If you liked the food, you can just end with a compliment.' Nikita smiled, glad that she made the effort to cook for Rajveer. 'If you called to tell me you liked the food, then it really must have been good. So, what is my bakshish for this, janab?' Nikita was fast picking up the local lingo.

Rajveer smiled. 'Should I come home to give you the sweet dish? You did not send ...' Rajveer, looking out of the window, smiled at the thought that, even though Nikita knew he would never come home during the day, she would still be blushing. He had not even completed the sentence when his attendant knocked at the door and entered.

'Jai Hind!'

Rajveer gave him a quick nod. 'Just hold on for a minute,' he said to Nikita.

'Sahab, you instructed me to inform you once the work at the computer centre was done. We just heard that it's complete,' the attendant said.

Rajveer nodded and said to Nikita, 'I'll call you later. Thanks again for the lovely lunch. Bye.' He then hung up and headed to the computer centre.

These were the moments in his job that gave Rajveer a high.

The electronic surveillance unit had hacked into a computer in the Lashkar-e-Taiba headquarters, and the best brains in the department had been going through the data on it.

Rajveer entered the computer room and a beaming hacker said, 'Sir, we've been successful.' The hacked computer revealed that the terrorist organization received at least Rs 10 crore every month. Lashkar had surplus money in hand and—from experience—Rajveer knew that this would be spent on recruitment, transport, training and supporting the families of terrorists that had been killed. Rajveer told his team to scrutinize each file on the hacked computer to get actionable intelligence on groups active in the Kashmir Valley. Any data on probable recruits, the location of training camps or the list of families of killed terrorists who were being funded by the Lashkar-e-Taiba would be extremely useful for counterterror operations in the Valley.

It was soon time for Nikita to head back to Delhi to rejoin her job. The couple decided to head to Noori Falls for a break before she made the journey. Legend had it that Noor Jahan used to bathe in these clear waters from the melting glacier. The falls are inside a cave and the story goes that Jehangir would watch his queen with the help of a well-placed mirror. The water in the falls was ice-cold. One could only wonder what material Noor Jahan was made of, to bathe in such cold waters. However, it did not really matter to the young couple. They put the water from the melting glacier to more practical use and chilled their beers, a gift to them from the army unit. It was the first drink they'd had together.

'Cheers!' Rajveer said as he raised his glass.

'Cheers to many more!' Nikita clicked her glass against Rajveer's.

They had a peaceful and romantic dinner that night. On the way to the airport though, there were moments of awkward silence, with neither of them knowing what to say. To ease the atmosphere a bit, Rajveer said, 'Summer in the Valley is very pleasant. We must plan a long vacation then. Try and work out your leave so we can take a break.'

Nikita looked at Rajveer and teasingly said, 'I can manage my leave; you speak for yourself.'

They started building castles in the air, planning their trip. Rajveer talked of the Pir Panjal range and the beauty of the place. He jokingly said, 'It's so pristine and beautiful only because tourists don't go there.'

The time to reach the airport is too short, thought Rajveer. He wished Nikita a safe journey, kissed her on her forehead, gave her a hug and stood there till he could no longer see her. Finally, he turned and headed back to his car.

The local commanders of Lashkar now had hundreds of recruits in the Kashmir Valley and were on the lookout for an exit route to take them into Pakistan for training by retired soldiers of the Pakistani army.

South Kashmir—comprising Pulwama, Anantnag and Kulgam—was close to Pir ki Gali on the Pir Panjal range, which had Poonch on the other side. Pir ki Gali was snowbound for six months during winter but opened up its passes and the beautiful seven lakes and meadows in summer. There were no visitors to this area since the terror activities had started, except the local Gujjars and Bakarwals, who had their *dhoks*—thatched huts used in summer—and *behaks*—private grazing land—in the higher reaches.

Commander Abu Hanzala, a man of Afghani origin, and his team of five Lashkar cadres set out that summer to look for the route that could take them across the border. They were equipped with AK assault rifles, Pika machine guns, grenades, rocket launchers and expensive Kenwood wireless sets. This was a standard kitty with the cadres of the rich Lashkar-e-Taiba. The Kenwood sets were so good that, from the top of the Pir Panjal range, they could contact their control station 'Alpha 3' across the Line of Control (LOC). The Pakistanis had powerful repeater stations all along the LOC to have a better communication network with the jihadis working in Jammu and Kashmir.

Standing at Pir ki Gali, Abu Hanzala took out a matrix sheet, wrote down a code, and sent a voice message across to Alpha 3—'A 22 BK 35 HHTP 241 KKIT'. Deciphered, the code read: 'We are looking out for a new route to take the recruits to Muzaffarabad via Poonch.'

The Lashkar control room replied: 'BB21 RR 24 51 46 84'. Which meant, 'Contact Md Yusuf at Fazlabad near Surankot.'

* * *

Surankot held a significant place in Rajveer's life. When he shared what happened at that place with Nikita, worry and anxiety immediately surfaced on her face. It was at Surankot that he'd had his first encounter in April 1998. However much you have prepared yourself for it, he told Nikita, the loss of a person hits you deeply, especially if it is someone as close as your personal security officer (PSO).

Rajveer's PSO, Abdul Qayoom, was a diligent and alert officer. He had developed a liking for Rajveer's clear and straightforward way of functioning. Qayoom was always eager to come forward and assist in whatever way he could.

Rajveer and his team had gone to Gunthal village having received specific information about the presence of terrorists there. As Rajveer stood on the roof of a house surveying the area, someone spoke on his wireless set. Terrorists had come on the police frequency and were challenging Rajveer. 'Where are you, Sir?' asked Ghuman Afghani, the local terrorist commander, who was much feared in that area.

'I am on the roof of Ibrahim's house,' replied Rajveer, knowing well that he was being observed by the terrorists.

Ibrahim was an ex-serviceman and Rajveer was confident that there would be no terrorist presence in his house.

'Look to your left and you will see me right across on the ridge line,' said Ghuman.

As soon as Rajveer looked left, Ghuman ran out of Ibrahim's house and began firing backwards with his Pika machine gun on his shoulder. Rajveer fired back but didn't get time to unfold his rifle butt. Despite their best efforts, they could not hit Ghuman. After five minutes of chasing, Rajveer gave up. He was too tired after having climbed the 2000 feet uphill to Gunthal, and could not keep pace with Ghuman, who was fresh after resting at Ibṛahim's house. When he walked back into the house, he saw Qayoom lying in a pool of blood.

'Alpha Quebec November Mike' (AQNM) was what Rajveer had transmitted to his headquarters. It meant that Abdul Qayoom was no more. The coded transmission was immediately understood and a condolence message had come back.

* * *

Now, Abu Hanzala walked down the old Mughal route— the route that the Mughal emperors would take from Delhi to Srinagar via Lahore. Pir ki Gali stood at 11,450 feet. It is said that Akbar used this route to Kashmir and, later, Jehangir used it when travelling for summer vacations. Two famous points on this route were the Chingus Sarai and the Aliabad Sarai. Legend had it that Jehangir died at Chingus Sarai, and they buried his intestines there. Innards are called *chingus* in Persian. His body was then embalmed and moved to Delhi. It was also at Pir ki Gali that Alexander's horse, Bucephalus, died from injuries suffered during the battle against Porus, which finally ended Alexander's dreams of world conquest. It is said that the place Buffliaz near Noori Falls got its name from Bucephalus.

It was almost as if the pir at Pir ki Gali reads the mind of whoever crosses the *gali*. If the person's designs are evil, the pir unleashes its power and destroys the evil-doer. The curse of the pir!

Abu Hanzala walked down the hill track from Pir Panjal to the remote village of Poshana and was greeted by the villagers. The local dish of doda, roti made of maize, and chicken was offered to the guests. Barely three weeks ago, a villager, Mohammed Sharief, had been beheaded by the cadres of the Hizbul Mujahideen Pir Panjal regiment (HMPPR) for being an informer. Thus, the entire village was subdued and ready to follow the dictates of the terrorists.

After halting there for a few hours, the team left for Dogrian, a village around three hours on foot from Poshana. Abu Hanzala and his team had planned to stay the night at Sailan, where they intended to meet the remaining members of the family of Imtiaz, the Hizbul Mujahideen commander of that area. Recently, some of their family were killed by a rival terror group trying to maintain their supremacy in the area. However, the family had placed the blame on security forces, primarily out of fear.

Now the Lashkar-e-Taiba had arrived. Such was the power of this group that commanders of both the warring factions came to meet and pay their respects to Abu Hanzala. Under his command, Zakir, the commander of the rival group, signed a *maafinama*, apologizing for killing the family members of Imtiaz. Their areas were then demarcated and responsibilities given to each for targeting security forces and informers. Recruitment for the LeT and establishing a permanent base for their operations at Behramgalla was their immediate task.

Chapter 5

Over the next few months, Nikita travelled to see Rajveer whenever she could. Back in Delhi, life would regain its regular maddening speed. Oh, how she missed the fresh air of Poonch and the tranquillity of the place. Now, all she could hear was the sound of the air conditioner and vehicles in the far background, a sharp contrast to the sound of silence—when there were no air attacks!—in the beautiful landscapes of Jammu and Kashmir.

She got into the rear seat of the car and told the driver to take her to her clinic. As the car moved smoothly through traffic, Nikita felt a bit restless. There was something not quite the way things should be with her stomach. Must be something she ate last night, she thought. She felt a little fatigued, too, and blamed it on the stomach bug. She closed her eyes to rest for a few minutes.

'Madam,' she could hear someone saying. She must be dreaming, she thought. 'Madam?'

Nikita realized it was not a dream. She had actually dozed off. They had reached the clinic and the driver was politely calling out to her. It was a bit strange, her dozing off, she thought, but quickly got out of the car and headed towards work and all that was waiting for her in the clinic. How she wished she could just grab a pillow and get some sleep.

Nikita got busy seeing her patients but was constantly reminded of her uneasiness because of persistent burping. At lunchtime, she decided to give her meal a miss. Five minutes later, she ordered a glass of buttermilk in the hope that it would ease her stomach. Sipping the cold and refreshing buttermilk, she dialled Rajveer's number. They had decided to chat while having lunch as often as they could. So, whenever she took a break for lunch, she would call him. If he, too, was having lunch at the same time, they would talk and eat together. He in Poonch and she in Delhi. Today, over lunch, they relived the time they had spent together in the beginning months of 2000 and their honeymoon trip to Pahalgam in the Kashmir Valley sponsored by their director general as a gift for their marriage.

Nikita continued to be restless for a few weeks. Now her stomach had settled but she was nauseous most of the time. She could barely eat. She was happy that Rajveer was in town though, and thought spending time with him would make things better. It did make things better.

Later that night, while they lay next to each other, she suddenly shrieked in a confused tone, 'Oh my God!'

'What happened?' Rajveer asked, unable to decipher if the shriek was a happy, sad, surprised or fearful one.

'When did we go to Pahalgam?'

'Last month,' Rajveer said.

'Looks like we are on our way to increasing the size of our family,' Nikita sheepishly said and buried her face in Rajveer's bare chest. She could not believe that she had missed her period and had not noticed it. Life can get so busy and beautiful at the same time, she thought gratefully.

Giving her a tight and warm hug, Rajveer smiled and it was decided that they would go to a doctor the next morning.

* * *

Hours later, on the other side of their world, Abu Hanzala and his team settled down for the night in Imtiaz's house. The Hizb cadres took turns to guard the house while the guests slept. Imtiaz's cousin, Afreen, dressed in her best outfit and with subtle make-up on, looked a bit more attractive than she really was. She was the one selected to keep company with the tall and handsome Afghani commander that night.

* * *

Sailan to Fazlabad was an hour's drive on the *kutcha* (unmetalled) track. On the way, though, they had to cross Buffliaz, the base camp of one company of 99 Para, a unit of the special forces. Such was the capability of this special forces unit that once, a wireless intercept by the police revealed, 'Don't cross Buffliaz. 99 Para commandos are there.'

Just a month ago, a small unit of 99 Para had raided a hideout of the Hizbul Mujahideen at Marha, killing five top cadres. To send a message, they decapitated the terrorists and paraded through the streets of Surankot town holding the five heads. It was clear to all overground workers of Surankot: any assistance to the terrorists would be dealt with as severely.

Abu Hanzala, having had a good night's rest, decided to walk the five hours towards Fazlabad, taking a detour to avoid the 99 Para camp. There, an overground worker, Mohammed Yusuf, was waiting. He took out his Kenwood set and passed on a coded message in Urdu to Alpha 3: '*Panchhi aa gaye, ghoda nahi liya.*' Alpha 3 was quick to decipher: 'Guests from far have arrived, but they did not take a vehicle to get here.'

Fazlabad is a village with a large base of Jamaat-e-Islami followers. Fundamentalists, they are naturally aligned with the jihadi ideology. Their support to the mujahideen was therefore more out of willingness than suppression.

Yusuf arranged for the guests to stay in five different houses of sympathizers to ensure that, in case of any adverse eventuality, the casualties would be minimal. This was standard procedure for the fundamentalists.

While Yusuf was handling the guests, Rajveer and his fellow officers were having a peaceful dinner at the Officers' Mess. Though they would meet to relax, work invariably found its way to the dinner table. They were sharing episodes when 'resources'—people who had family on both sides of the border and who would be willing to give information for a sum—would give some completely inconsequential information and walk off with the money. But this was a gamble the department had to take because there would also be episodes when the resource would give specific details to the extent that encounters could be based on them. It was a good space to be in, Rajveer thought—

where you could share your stories and learn from others. As it always happened when officers met socially, the topic moved from strategizing to gossip. As they parted to retire for the night, they shared rumours about prospective transfers. Anyone who could claim authority on the topic was considered to be a champion in 'internal intelligence'. The standing joke, however, was that the rumours got to know that they were rumours, and therefore never came true.

The next day, while Rajveer went on with the daily meetings with the Special Analysis Wing (SAW) and his own subordinates, Yusuf discussed modalities.

The distance from Shopian in Kashmir to the Lashkar headquarters and training camp at Muzaffarabad via Poonch and Mendhar would take at least four or five days on foot. They, therefore, needed two transit camps. Hill Kaka was chosen as the first one. It was a densely forested valley protected by mountain ranges. The advantage of this place from a terrorist's point of view was the fact that it was a day's trek from the nearest roadhead in the Kashmir Valley, it was full of natural caves—which made it perfect for hideouts—it had plenty of wild animals that could be hunted to feed the camping mujahideen and, most importantly, it was at least a two-day trek from any security force camp in Surankot. They simply had to position observation parties with wireless sets on top of the surrounding mountains to forewarn them about any security force movement. As an additional cover, they had a large number of Bakarwal dogs. These dogs were ferocious, much more even than German Shepherds. The Bakarwalis used them to keep watch on their sheep herds.

They claimed that one dog was sufficient to watch over a hundred sheep.

Having decided on Hill Kaka as the first stop, Yusuf and Abu Hanzala settled on Hari Budha in the Surankot area and Gursai in the Mendhar area as the next two transit camps. These too were safe from the security angle, and the mujahideen had to travel for only around twelve to fourteen hours to reach these places from the nearest point on the LOC.

Having settled this, Abu Hanzala headed back to Kashmir with the help of local guides. Overground workers were put to work to shift rations, blankets and other logistics to make living in these areas comfortable.

* * *

By the early part of the year 2000, the Lashkar-e-Jabbar had recruited local Kashmiri boys in large numbers. Though primarily a Pakistani Deobandi outfit, the Lashkar-e-Jabbar needed local support to sustain its activities in the Valley. Created with the support of the ISI, the Lashkar-e-Jabbar had all the resources to recruit and train jihadis on the scale of the Taliban, but they too needed to exfiltrate new recruits from the Valley and infiltrate the trained ones. The transit camps that LeT had set up at Hill Kaka, Hari Budha and Gursai would now serve any terror outfit that wanted to use them. All of them—be it LeT, Lashkar-e-Jabbar, Al-Badr or Hizbul Mujahideen—kept their representatives as caretakers for the transiting groups whether they were new recruits exfiltrating to Pakistan or trained recruits moving from Pakistan to the Kashmir Valley.

War stores were dumped by all the terror groups in their respective hideouts. One side of the Hill Kaka valley was kept exclusively as a firing range to practise with different kinds of weapons. A natural cave was used to practise short-distance firing with pistols. Rations, kerosene oil, dry eatables, stoves and utensils were all available to whichever group wanted to use them. Abu Umer, a jihadi who had suffered serious bullet injuries to his leg during an encounter in the Kashmir Valley, offered to be the cashier and maintained accounts of all the groups. He had completely dedicated himself to the jihadi cause. Ponies and horses were kept in reserve to shift heavy machinery—rocket launchers, Pika machine guns and grenade launchers were too heavy and needed animal transport. They were also sometimes used by the commanders located there when they went out hunting. In short, Hill Kaka was a jihadi village sufficient in all aspects. So much so that even the locals who went about their daily work supported the jihadis.

Once, Rajveer led a team for operations towards Hill Kaka. They were served tea by a local from the village. The tea-seller was a multifaceted character. He not only served tea but, even with his limited formal education, was a poet in his own right. His poetry had abundant humour and kept Rajveer and his team entertained and relaxed. The team generously complimented his talent and expressed their appreciation for his having maintained equanimity in such adverse conditions.

They later learnt that the clever poet, in the garb of humorous poetry, was buying time so that three terrorists hiding in his own house could move quietly to the nearby jungle. Such was the village of Hill Kaka!

Over the next year and a half, terror activity reached its peak in the Kashmir Valley. The Lashkar-e-Jabbar in particular adopted the Taliban style of operations against security forces and against strategic targets. In October 2001, they exploded a car bomb outside the J&K Legislative Assembly. Emboldened by their first major attack, they then carried out a suicide attack at the Indian Parliament in December 2001. The terror highway of Muzaffarabad–Poonch/Mendhar–Hari Budha/Gursai–Hill Kaka–Pir ki Gali–Shopian–Kashmir Valley established by Abu Hanzala was now in full use. The sparsely located security force deployment was not enough to put a stop to the infiltration of terrorists.

The government took immediate action and the then Union interior minister, Trishna Motwani, called for a high-level meeting at the North Block in New Delhi to consider ways to stop infiltration. A two-pronged strategy was discussed in the meeting. It was decided that, first, they had to give a decisive blow to the transit camp at Hill Kaka. And second, they would need to fence the LOC. The decision was made to focus on the former, first. An attack on the transit camp would not only inflict casualties on the terror groups but would also cause a major dent to the terror highway. Two army brigades comprising at least 5000 personnel would be involved. The police were roped in for ground support and specific intelligence. Intelligence developed by the local superintendent of police, Rajveer Singh, revealed a sizeable presence of at least three groups at Hill Kaka: the Lashkar-e-Jabbar, with around fifteen cadres including ten fresh recruits; the LeT, with thirty cadres; and the HMPPR, with thirty cadres. Others included skeletal staff of the Al-Badr and the Hizbul Mujahideen. Intel also revealed the presence of Moulvi Anayatulla of Shopian, who was in charge of religious preaching for all the cadres together.

* * *

Back in Jammu, a helicopter reconnaissance was launched over Hill Kaka with the senior superintendent of police and commanding officer of 99 Para on board. Through high-powered binoculars, they could easily see smoke coming out of a cookhouse and people moving around on horseback. It was clear that the security forces were in for a rich haul.

A large-scale operation was planned at the Tango Force Headquarters of the Army, in which senior police officers and intelligence officers would participate. One full brigade along with the police was to be deployed to carry out the operation. First, teams would be sent on foot to cover all the villages and valley exit routes surrounding Hill Kaka. This would require an overnight journey on foot. Even if the observation parties noticed the movement, the terrorists were unlikely to move out since they were far from where the militants were. They were also confident that they would be able to escape into the surrounding mountain ridges and forests. However, they were not aware that forces would be heli-dropped, covering all the mountain ridges around to completely seal the exit routes. Even if the terrorists finally did get a hint of the operation being launched, it would be very difficult for them to come out of the cordon. Those deployed had sufficient survival rations—readymade eatables and an improvised store—to survive for at least two days without reinforcements.

The search operation was launched and, in the first assault, nine terrorists were killed and there was a rich haul of weapons and logistics supplies. To the surprise of the forces, they saw that concrete bunkers had been made to protect the terrorists from aerial assault. Six mobile phones were recovered at a time when mobiles had not even started functioning in Poonch. Of what use were these to the terrorists then? Maulvi Anayatullah of Shopian had the answer to this. He was the only terrorist who had been apprehended. The rest had either been killed or managed to escape. Anayatullah informed the forces that, whenever the terrorists wanted to make a call, they would climb to the highest ridge near Hill Kaka. From there, they could make a direct call to the high-power mobile towers installed at Forward Kahuta across Poonch and at Nakyal across Mendhar. Kahuta was at an aerial distance of 11.5 km, whereas Nakyal was around 14 km from Hill Kaka.

A large number of matrix sheets were also recovered from the hideouts, which were immediately referred to the Signals division to be deciphered. However, by the time they could be used to intercept terrorists, the control room at POK had changed the codes and issued fresh ones. This was one matter that the terrorists attended to on top priority since it was a matter of life and death for them.

At the end of the seven-day operation, a total of thirty-seven terrorists were killed. Those who escaped from ground zero at Hill Kaka were trapped by the forces on the outer cordon while attempting to flee. Operation Purna Vinash at Hill Kaka was a grand success. It dismantled the terror highway infrastructure that had taken almost a year to build and stock up and, more importantly, eliminated key commanders from all groups.

The second part of the strategy adopted during the meeting chaired by the interior minister was greatly facilitated by the success of the first part. It immediately brought down infiltration figures.

Ground inputs from intelligence agencies had suggested that fencing the LOC would be of immense help. Finance clearance was given to the project and, immediately after Operation Purna Vinash, material was dumped at the site and construction of the fence started on a war footing. The army started with a demonstration fencing on two stretches, one in Mendhar and the other in Poonch. Such was the importance given to this project that Mr Motwani himself flew to the Balakot sector in Mendhar to inspect the fence.

By the time the terror groups recouped after the beating at Hill Kaka, the fence at the LOC was almost ready. The gaps in the fence arising out of *nallahs* (water channels) were covered with improvised methods. Ambushes were laid in depth areas covering vulnerable points. With the intervention of technology and the establishment of the fence, Indian forces were now in a much better position to prevent infiltration.

The Lashkar-e-Jabbar now had to think of other ways to send in trained men.

Chapter 6

Rajveer and Nikita both wanted a girl. Nikita always imagined buying clothes for her daughter, dressing her up and eventually becoming friends with her as their shoe sizes started matching. Rajveer did not know why, but he wanted a daughter too.

Waiting outside the operation theatre with Rajveer were Nikita's mother and her sister Payal. After some time, the doctor came out and, with a huge smile, said, 'It was a normal delivery and both mother and daughter are fine.'

Daughter! Did he say 'daughter'? Rajveer had the biggest grin on his face when he thanked the doctor and asked when was it possible to see both of them. 'In a while, we will inform you,' the doctor said, before vanishing behind the sheer glass door of the OT.

'I knew! I just knew it! Didi always gets what she wants,' Payal said, grinning.

Three days after the delivery, Nikita was discharged and returned home. She saw that Rajveer had placed a vase filled with flowers in their room; there was fresh bed linen and some soft toys on the bed. She smiled at her husband's eagerness to impress their just-born daughter but loved the gesture. Exhausted, she decided to rest while the baby slept.

Aakriti, Sonal, Sumegha, Anvik, Ishaani . . . Everyone in the family gave their suggestions on the best name for the lovely new addition to the family. Everyone also shared their opinion as to who the baby most resembled.

It was finally decided that her name would be Aakriti Singh, and she resembled only herself.

Soon, however, Rajveer had to return to his posting while Nikita and Aakriti continued to stay in Delhi. It took a lot of effort for Rajveer to leave the two of them behind— he had somehow begun to experience a facet of himself that he did not know existed. He wanted to be with his daughter, to rock her to sleep and watch her sleeping. He wanted to watch her smile in her sleep. He wanted to be around to see her give that sleepy yawn, and look at things with great curiosity. He just wanted to be able to see her every day. But that was not possible, he knew. He had a duty to fulfil and that meant he had to be in a different state.

Back in Jammu, life for Rajveer moved at an oxymoronic hasty-slow speed. His time in office went by in a blur, with all the strategizing and planning needed, while his time in his house in Jammu moved slower than ever before. Sitting in his room now, Rajveer looked at his watch and wondered what the two girls in his life were doing. How time passes when you are with your loved ones, he thought. He aimlessly walked around his house, not knowing what to do with himself. He picked up the hourglass on the fireplace mantel and flipped it around a couple of times.

In a safe house at Defence Colony in Karachi, a heated argument was taking place between Brig. Mohammed Aslam of the ISI and Maulana Majid Asgar.

A few days ago, sitting at the Lashkar-e-Jabbar headquarters at Bahawalpur, Maulana Asgar had contacted his controllers at the ISI to discuss alternative ways to provide men and material to the depleting strength of the mujahideen in the Kashmir Valley. A meeting had been organized in Karachi with Brig. Aslam, who was in charge of the Kashmir division within the ISI. The maulana brought up the problem at hand, but Brig. Aslam countered this with a barrage of questions.

'Why did you attack the convoy of President Musharraf?' Brig. Aslam asked Maulana Asgar.

'We did not attack the convoy,' Maulana Asgar replied with a straight face.

'Everyone in Pakistan knows you did it, and nothing in Pakistan escapes the eye of the ISI. Do you understand?' Brig. Aslam said.

At this juncture, Maulana Asgar did what he was best at. He cited verses from the Quran.

'Fa-izza Azemta fata-Wakkelallaullah
Inna ulla ha Yuhibbu-ul mutawakkeleen.'

[Trust in Allah when making decisions. Then when you have taken a decision, put your trust in Allah. Certainly, Allah loves those who put their trust in him.]

He continued,

'Walal Aakhiratu Khairul lakaminaloola.'

[Indeed, what is to come will be better for you than what has gone by.]

Brig. Aslam was hesitant to extend immediate support to the Lashkar-e-Jabbar. 'There is a lot of pressure on us to take action against the Lashkar-e-Jabbar after the attack on the Indian Parliament,' he said.

Aslam explained how much effort it had taken to shift focus from the Lashkar-e-Taiba and to start supporting the Lashkar-e-Jabbar. The LeT had ventured into areas that were unsanctioned by the ISI and invited international wrath. Their dummy NGO, which the ISI used to fund them, had been exposed during Indian investigations and, as a result, the LeT was proscribed as a terrorist organization. The Lashkar-e-Jabbar was supported to overcome this problem. The attack on the Indian Parliament could not achieve the desired results, and all the effort to shift the blame to the LeT in this attack was futile after Afzal Guru was arrested and investigations led to Rana Tahir Nadeem, alias Ghazi Baba, alias Abu Jihadi, who hailed from Bahawalpur, the home town of Maulana Asgar, who was the chief of the Lashkar-e-Jabbar in the Kashmir Valley at that time.

However, the maulana was adamant. After all, the Lashkar-e-Jabbar was a part of the larger design of the ISI itself.

Finally, Brig. Aslam and Maulana Asgar reached an agreement. The ISI would now use their fake Indian currency notes smuggling infrastructure in Bangladesh and Nepal to push in Lashkar-e-Jabbar cadres to India. The printing of fake Indian currency notes in Pakistan with government currency printing machines and smuggling them into India via Nepal and Bangladesh was part of the design of the ISI to weaken India's economic stability. It was also part of the initial plan of General Zia-ul-Haq to bleed India through a thousand cuts.

'Although, officially, we have to proscribe your organization in Pakistan for terror acts in India as well as the attack on President Musharraf, we will continue to support and fund you to achieve our ultimate aim of annexing Kashmir to Pakistan,' Brig. Aslam said finally. It would require a lot of finances, which the ISI was already providing. 'In no circumstance do we land up like the LeT,' Brig. Aslam said.

Maulana Asgar went back to Bahawalpur and held a meeting with his top commanders to tell them about the new plan. All of them agreed that, with the support of the ISI unit at Kathmandu, this was a safe method of sending in as many mujahideen as possible. They, however, raised the issue of finance and logistics support once the mujahideen reached Jammu and Kashmir.

Maulana Asgar had anticipated this and had a reply ready. 'To take care of the finances, we will establish an NGO that will serve as a front to receive donations.' Through this organization, they could receive money in the form of *zakat* as well as from the ISI and the oil-rich countries. 'Al Khidmat', meaning 'mercy', was the name suggested by one of the commanders, Musa.

The maulana was inspired by the LeT's Falah-e-Insaniyat (FIF) foundation, which overtly did charity, such as supporting earthquake victims, providing medical care through their ambulances, etc., but covertly was a front for funds to the LeT. On the ground, FIF ambulances were used to ferry maulvis who would spot young talent in the villages, and then the same ambulances carried new recruits to the Muridke camp in Lahore for the three stages of training they received before they were taken into Jammu and Kashmir: 'Daura-e-Talba', 'Daura-e-Aam' and the 'Daura-e-Khas'. Daura-e-Talba included morning physical exercise, religion class and light weapons training. Daura-e-Aam included a second round of the same schedule with enhanced weapons training and firing practice. Daura-e-Khas was the final round of training, which included advanced weapons training, map reading, tactical training and night firing.

Terror outfits like the Lashkar-e-Jabbar had simply copied the LeT model and started recruiting and training in similar ways. The only difference between the Lashkar-e-Jabbar and the LeT was the strong connection the former had with the Taliban and Al-Qaeda. Unlike the LeT— which used retired ISI majors, subedars and havildars— the Lashkar-e-Jabbar got ready trainers from the Taliban who were war-hardened. They also sent their best cadres to Afghanistan to train with the Taliban in their training facilities.

Another big difference was their emphasis on religious teachings. While the LeT focused 80 per cent of their time on combat training and 20 per cent on religious teachings, Maulana Asgar insisted on maintaining a 60:40 ratio. He kept 60 per cent of the time for religious texts and 40 per cent for combat training. His firm opinion was that, 'Once a Lashkar-e-Jabbar cadre is convinced about the path he is following, Allah gives him the strength to fight.' A set of maulvis that had studied under Maulana Asgar himself trained the recruits at the training camp.

Soon, infiltrations started from the alternative route suggested by the ISI. Khursheed Ahmed, aka Chacha, was stationed with an ISI officer at the Pakistani embassy in Kathmandu. Mohammed Yunous, aka Langda, was stationed at Dhaka. It was the job of the ISI to get valid passports and visas for the recruits. The ISI desk at Karachi hired a dormitory in the city for recruits. They would rest and recuperate there, and Maulana Zaif, Maulana Asgar's brother, would do the briefing and talk to them about their responsibilities. A large screen was installed in the conference hall at the transit camp to explain to the recruits about the route to be taken and the names and contacts of Lashkar-e-Jabbar cadres who would receive them at Dhaka, Kathmandu and at the borders of Bangladesh and Nepal with India. Manzoor Trali naturally figured as the most important connect in India. The recruits were told about important Lashkar-e-Jabbar strongholds in the Kashmir Valley and shown these places on Google Maps.

* * *

Manzoor Trali, though in prison at the time, had enough followers in Kashmir to facilitate the movement of Lashkar-e-Jabbar cadres from Nepal and Bangladesh. He had access to a mobile phone that had been smuggled inside the jail after paying a handsome amount to the guard commander. He also got a doctor posted inside the sub-hospital on the jail premises who was a distant relative. Whenever he had to communicate with his

followers, he went to the sub-hospital for a check-up
and made a call from the doctor's chamber. He sent
one trusted lieutenant, Ashfaq Ahmed, to the Binapole
border in Bangladesh and another, Imran Khan, to the
Raxaul border in Nepal to coordinate the infiltrations.
Both Ashfaq and Imran were old associates of his and had
been in jail earlier. They had been released after having
served their five-year sentences for providing overground
support to terrorists.

The borders were porous and almost the entire
population at Malda in West Bengal and Forbesganj in Bihar
was deeply involved with fake Indian currency smuggling.
The Lashkar-e-Jabbar hired a hotel each at Forbesganj and
Malda to take care of the transit requirements. Although
they arrived with valid passports and visas in Bangladesh
and Nepal, they were told to deposit this with Langda
and Chacha at the respective locations. They were then
issued fake Indian identity cards with Hindu names before
crossing the international border. Instructions were clear.
All those infiltrating had to be clean-shaven as per the
custom for fidayeen—it was considered a mark of extreme
devotion and personal purity. They were also asked to wear
the red thread or tilak worn by Hindus, but some of them
refused to do this because of their religious beliefs.

Infiltrations started in good numbers. It was now
important to manage the finances. Zafarullah Azad, a
local chartered accountant based in Pulwama, who had
earlier managed the accounts of the Jammu and Kashmir
Liberation Front (JKLF) and was an expert in creating
fake accounts and bills, was appointed the treasurer
and the accountant. He started running a magazine,
Inqalaab, and showed huge amounts of funds received for

advertisements. Some companies did send in money for advertisements, but the amounts shown in the receipts were much larger than had actually come in. Funds collected from the ISI were thus disguised. Zafarullah also created a local NGO called the Al Shafa Trust, which on paper was set up to look after destitute children who had lost their parents to terror activity. Asifa, Manzoor Trali's wife, was appointed as the chairperson of the trust to give it a more humane look. For all practical purposes, the Al-Shafa Trust was the local counterpart of the Al-Khidmat Trust. So well did Zafarullah disguise the activities of his trust that even the state government donated Rs 10 lakh every year to it.

However, more funds were needed than the small amounts of money received through *hawala*, and Zafarullah eyed the cross-border trade as the best channel to get it.

This cross-border trade was a barter system started by former chief minister Mufti Hameed in 2003 under the leadership of Sajal Vajpayee in order to create goodwill between India and Pakistan. In this process, goods of equivalent amounts were exchanged by traders of the two countries. Money did not exchange hands, but the trader could sell the goods he received locally and earn a good profit. Thus, products like almonds and walnuts, produced in abundance in Pakistan, came to India, and bananas and spices would go from India to Pakistan.

Zafarullah created a company called Zafar and Associates, which would supply cashew nuts, morels, cardamom, bananas and a host of other goods to Pakistan through the Chakoti border trade route. Business began and was a huge success. It was an idea that was sure to fill the coffers of the Lashkar-e-Jabbar.

Zafarullah's manoeuvre did not go unnoticed by Hamad Lone, though. Hamad Lone was the minister in charge of trade and industries and he controlled most of the border trade. The profits were huge, and a large amount of the money went towards funds for his party, the People's Democratic Forum (PDF).

Irked, Hamad Lone sent his brother Babar with gunmen to Zafarullah's house in downtown Srinagar to ask him to shut down the company and keep away from the border trade business. To Babar's surprise, a larger posse of gunmen, heavily armed, greeted them. These were Lashkar-e-Jabbar cadres. Babar kept his cool. He asked his gunmen to stay outside the gate and started talking to Zafarullah. Instead of asking Zafarullah to stop his activities, he offered him a partnership.

'Although we do not allow anyone to enter our field of business, we understand the cause of holy jihad and the contribution of the Lashkar-e-Jabbar to the Kashmir cause. We can reserve trading in bananas and cardamom for Zafar and Associates,' Babar said.

'What else can we keep? You are offering too little and the organization needs more money,' Zafarullah said.

'Janab, the local businessmen will suffer,' Babar said.

'No suffering is more than the suffering faced by the Kashmiris. While you have a narrow lens through which you look at the picture, the Lashkar-e-Jabbar is working for all the Kashmiris,' Zafarullah said.

'Janab, what else do you need?' Babar asked.

'We need regular arms and ammunition supplies for our men,' Zafarullah said.

Thus, it was agreed that cavities would be built in some of the trucks, where weapons could be safely hidden and smuggled. One out of every ten trucks coming in would bring in weapons.

The deal was settled without the use of force. Babar retreated with his gunmen and went back to Handwara. When he told his brother what had happened, Hamad was furious.

'Our finances will fall by at least 25 per cent,' he said.

'There is no point confronting the Lashkar-e-Jabbar,' Babar said. 'Besides, we can figure out alternative sources.'

'Like what?' Hamad asked.

'Pakistan supplies drugs to the entire world. Why can't they supply it to us in the name of helping the Lashkar-e-Jabbar?' Babar said.

'But will the Lashkar-e-Jabbar agree to the narcotics business?' Hamad asked. 'Does it not go against the fundamentals of the Deobandi ideology?'

'The Taliban also did it. They follow the same ideology,' Babar said. 'When it comes down to getting finances to run the organization, compromises are made.'

But when Babar made a call to Zafarullah, he refused outright. 'It's a sin,' he said.

Babar hung up and thought, 'Is it necessary to tell them that narcotics are coming in? Why can't we control the movement of their trucks and bring in drugs in concealed spaces, just like the arms and ammunition? If the drugs are discovered by the police, Zafar and Associates will bear the brunt. If the drugs get through, the profit is all ours.'

Babar and Hamad discussed the modalities.

Meanwhile, the ISI brigadier had another idea by which the Lashkar-e-Jabbar could get money.

The invoices for goods that Zafar and Associates transported from Pakistan to India would be under-invoiced by at least 50 per cent. So, only goods worth the amount on the invoice would be returned from India in the barter system. The rest, in cash, would be available for the Lashkar-e-Jabbar to use in Kashmir. Zafarullah would camouflage this surplus money through the magazine, *Inqalaab*.

The result was simple. Without having to involve hawala traders and without any wire transfers from Pakistan, the Lashkar-e-Jabbar had plenty of money in Kashmir. The ISI suffered the losses caused by the arrangement, which they made available out of funds earmarked for jihad in Kashmir. An estimate of the total amount of funds available for the Lashkar-e-Jabbar out of border trade during a later investigation by the Terror Investigation Agency (TIA), the elite counterterror investigation agency, pegged it at around Rs 100 crore.

Of course, Zafarullah could not have kept such large amounts of cash, so he diverted it to 'corporate social responsibility' and benevolently donated huge amounts of profit earned in their trade business to the Al Shafa Trust. The bank accounts of the trust now had healthy deposits that looked genuine. The Lashkar-e-Jabbar continued to build its cadre strength using this money.

Hideouts were created in hundreds of houses in south Kashmir. Arms were smuggled through the trade route in plenty. Emboldened by the increase in the number of hardcore, well-trained jihadis, and equipped with assault rifles, rocket launchers, grenade launchers and improvised explosive devices, the Lashkar-e-Jabbar carried out two deadly attacks. In the first, they attacked the Baramulla brigade. A group of four freshly infiltrated terrorists from the Baramulla sector carried out a suicide attack. They planned it at a time when the exchange of forces was taking place and the new battalion was replacing the old one. As a result, many of the forces were put up in tented accommodation. The casualties were, therefore, on the higher side.

The second attack was at the police lines at Anantnag. Two terrorists struck in the early morning hours when policemen had assembled for namaz. Due to the prevailing security scenario, all police personnel preferred to offer namaz at the police lines. While they were offering namaz, one of the terrorists threw a grenade at the bunker of a policeman guarding the family quarters. As soon as the guard was neutralized, the terrorists entered Block A of the family quarters. An encounter followed, in which five members of families of policemen suffered casualties and the two suicide attackers were killed.

Killing the two suicide attackers was good, but losing family members of the policemen gave people in the branch reason to talk about Rajveer. Jealousy is a powerful emotion, and Rajveer felt it in the steam bath at the gym the next morning. Rajveer was very particular about his own physical fitness as well as that of his entire team. To lead by example, he was a regular at the gym, which always ended with a session in the steam bath. It not only enhanced the effect of the exercise, but it was also a chance to meet like-minded people and catch up on the gossip. Officers often met there by chance and the exchange of juicy stories would keep them there for longer than the desired duration. The fogginess created by the steam was no deterrent to the officers; in fact, it was even more fun because one could say whatever was on their mind and get away with it, leaving fellow officers guessing about the identity of the speaker.

The steam bath was also where strategies were sometimes informally discussed. That morning, Rajveer entered the bath with Anantnag on his mind and would have discussed it with someone he trusted, had he found them. The bath was very foggy that morning, and he could not identify anyone clearly. He chose a quiet corner and let the pores of his body open and relax. Just when his mind and body were getting in sync and decompressing, he heard something that caught his attention.

'What do you feel about the Anantnag encounter?' someone asked.

'What do I think? I think nothing. I don't think of such people,' said a second voice.

As if wanting to add fuel to the fire, a third voice asked, 'Which people?'

The second man was quick to respond. 'The likes of Rajveer. The guy doesn't know how to treat his subordinates. All he is good at is getting our own people killed.'

Rajveer did not need this that morning. He remembered what his grandfather once told him: *Jab haathi chalte hain toh kutte bhaukte hain*—when someone goes out there to do a good job or takes up a big project, the small fry bark like dogs. He left the bath without saying anything. He had work to do!

Chapter 7

One person who came back through the Nepal route after successfully completing the Baramulla and Anantnag police lines attacks was Abdul Rehman Qadri, aka ARQ. He was around forty years old and was more of a mentor, guide and planner of ground operations in the Kashmir Valley. After having spent the mandatory three years in the Valley and having achieved some of the biggest successes, he had earned his return to Pakistan. Very few mujahids returned—most were eliminated before they completed their tenure. ARQ was one of the lucky ones. And he had proven his worth by not only completing three years in the Valley but with the distinction of having coordinated the Baramulla brigade and Anantnag police lines attack.

Soon after his return, he was moved to the Lashkar-e-Jabbar headquarters at Bahawalpur as the chief coordinator. He was given charge of recruitment, training and launching of mujahids, besides being the administrator at the Bahawalpur headquarters, replacing Afzal Ahmed, who had become old and was no longer able to manage the affairs of the Lashkar-e-Jabbar headquarters efficiently.

ARQ would also organize the Friday prayer congregation at the Lashkar-e-Jabbar headquarters, where the maulanas Asgar and Zaif would address huge gatherings, and took care of the core security of the two brothers. His sincerity and dedication to jihad were such that he would work full-time at the headquarters and rarely took leave to visit home and family. He was a tough taskmaster and knew how to extract the maximum from everyone. Over the next six months, he would establish himself as the most powerful and most feared Lashkar-e-Jabbar commander at the headquarters.

* * *

After the Baramulla brigade and Anantnag police lines attacks, Pakistan denied any involvement and issued a press release stating that the Indian government was unnecessarily dragging their name into it, while the attacks were the work of local Kashmiris dedicated to the cause of freedom.

Things were changing at Rajveer's end too. He was transferred to Delhi as inspector general of the counterterror organization, TIA. It was a welcome move for Nikita; she was happy they could now finally be together for longer durations of time, and Aakriti would get to see her father more. Rajveer too was excited to be focusing more on investigative work. He could apply the learning that he had received from his counterparts in the US.

As luck would have it, the investigation into the Anantnag police lines attack was of such importance that the Central government assigned a team of the elite TIA to the case. At the same time, the director general of the TIA entrusted the investigation into the Baramulla attack, which had so far hit a dead end, to Rajveer. Instructions were clear. The TIA had to find evidence to establish the involvement of Pakistan-based terrorists in the attack.

A special Air Force C7 Hercules took off from Ghaziabad Airbase with a team of fifteen ace investigators. They collected evidence from the scene of the attacks at Anantnag. A part of the same team revisited the evidence collected so far in the Baramulla attack case and found some Bangladeshi and Nepali numbers written on a piece of paper recovered from the pocket of one of the terrorists who was killed. A special electronic surveillance unit was deployed by the TIA to work on these numbers.

Nikita and Rajveer were house hunting, checking out homes that were vacant and on offer to the new inspector general of TIA. They finally saw something they both loved. It was on the ground floor, which promised sunlight and had a modest lawn. Just as they were sitting in the car, physically exhausted from the whole exercise but finally mentally relaxed, Rajveer's phone rang. It was his office. 'Sir, the numbers are of foreign origin and cannot be intercepted directly.'

'I'll call Parth,' Rajveer said and disconnected. Parth was the computer geek who had helped them to crack the case of Asif Majeed, an ISIS terrorist in Mumbai, who was later sent back to Syria. Parth had unravelled a mysterious maze of calls and zeroed in on the users of Twitter handles operated by ISIS. Parth was an expert at gaming and hacking and was popularly called StOrM in the hacking community.

'Where are you?' asked Rajveer when Parth answered. He could tell Parth was not in the country from the different ringtone.

'Holidaying in Seychelles,' Parth replied. 'Anything urgent?'

'We need you in Kashmir for an important investigation,' Rajveer said, adding that he couldn't give details since he was calling from his mobile phone.

'Give me ten minutes. Meanwhile, switch to the Dialog app and turn the message destroy option to five seconds,' Parth said.

Parth had been by the pool when Rajveer called. Now, he pulled on a bathrobe and hurried to his room. He switched on his personal installation of an open VPN to mask his traffic on the hotel's Wi-Fi and called Rajveer on Dialog.

'Tell me,' Parth said.

'We're investigating the attack on the brigade headquarters at Baramulla. We have some Bangladesh and Nepal numbers which have definite links with the terrorists responsible. We need your help cracking them,' Rajveer said.

Parth immediately had a solution. 'See, international calls to Bangladesh and Nepal are routed through our telecom service providers, and even though they may be voice or data calls, they have the Internet Protocol gateways to traverse. Try identifying the specific IP addresses used for calls to Nepal and Bangladesh and use pattern analysis. The task is difficult but definitely not impossible.'

'Understood,' Rajveer said. 'We'll get in touch with the Digital Analysis Unit (DAU) right away.'

When Rajveer called the Digital Analysis Unit of the Interior Ministry, they came up with an interception solution and the numbers recovered from the Baramulla attack site hit pay dirt.

'Adnan bhai is coming via the Sanauli border. Send Imran there to receive,' revealed the intercept of the Nepali number.

TIA contacted their mole with the Nepali telecom service provider and asked for the address linked to the Nepali number. Within minutes, it was on Rajveer's table. Sheikh Amjad, House at Plot No. 37, Belahiya, Sanauli.

* * *

'I'm going to be away on tour for a few days,' Rajveer told Nikita when he got home that evening.

'How long will you be gone?'

'I don't really know. A couple of days. Maybe two.'

Nikita smiled and nodded. She was used to waiting for him for days together; two days seemed very doable. She was wondering when to break the news to him. That night, when they retired for the day, she quietly but very happily told him that Aakriti was going to have a sibling. It was a happy moment for both of them.

'Why didn't you tell me in the evening? We could have had a drink to celebrate,' Rajveer said.

'IG sahib, now no drinks for at least a year, if not more!' Nikita was quick to respond.

'Only for you. I am a free bird,' Rajveer was quicker to reply.

Nikita punched him lightly, laughing.

The next morning, Rajveer left early. Before he did, he hugged Nikita, and as he usually did before leaving on tour, he reminded her to not call him—he would call her.

Along with a team of the TIA and a strike team of the Special Security Guard (SSG), Rajveer headed towards the border. The target—Sheikh Amjad's house—was about 3 km into Nepal territory.

The team was stopped at the Sanauli border by the Defence Service Bureau Guards that manned the Indo–Nepal border. 'Where are you guys heading to at eleven in the night?' the guard commander asked.

Rajveer and his team had decided to carry out the mission undercover, so they were in civilian clothes and travelling in two luxury sedans. The weapons were hidden. Rajveer was dressed like a wealthy Marwari and was even wearing a heavy gold chain. In the typical manner of a wealthy man who thinks everything can be bought, Rajveer handed over an envelope full of Rs 1000 notes.

'We'll be back in a few hours. Some important business,' he said, in a commanding tone because the envelope had exchanged hands.

The guard commander went back to the barracks and the teams moved on.

Explains how the groups keep entering so easily, Rajveer thought to himself.

The teams reached Sheikh Amjad's home at midnight. It was a modest house with a six-foot-tall brick wall built around the boundary. It was close to a densely forested area—an ideal place to host terrorists. They could escape to the forests in case of a raid.

Rajveer and his team quietly jumped the wall and knocked at the door. No response. With the idea of not giving Sheikh Amjad any time to escape, they broke open the door and saw a couple, one of whom was Amjad, caught with his pants down, literally. The two looked at the intruders in disbelief, before the man hurriedly put on his pants, and the woman headed towards the washroom, grabbing her clothes, trying to protect her modesty.

The SSG team commander grabbed hold of Amjad and put his hand on his mouth. The others stormed through the house, searching every inch of it. The woman emerged fully clothed from the washroom and was asked to sit in a corner and keep her mouth shut. She lowered her head and did as she was told.

Rajveer began to ask Amjad questions, armed with the information they had from intercepting calls. Perhaps realizing that he had no choice, Amjad began to talk.

'Adnan bhai will reach here any time soon,' he said. 'The local guide, Chacha, will be with them. Imran is in the makeshift hideout in the nearby forests; he will come here when he gets the code "mandir".'

'How long have you been doing this?' asked Rajveer.

'For many years now,' Amjad said. 'I must have received at least twenty groups so far.'

'Which organization do you work for?'

'Lashkar-e-Jabbar,' Amjad replied. He said the generous doles of money out of the Lashkar-e-Jabbar exchequer had made him an '*ayyash*'—addicted to pleasure.

The team got hold of the wireless set used by Amjad and waited for Adnan bhai. Rajveer set the wireless frequency to 147.45, as revealed by Amjad, and sent out the code 'mandir' to Imran.

'Ji janab,' came the reply from Imran.

In what seemed to be very little time, Rajveer and his team spotted Imran approaching the house. They pinned him down at the gate itself. Catching such an important operative alive was an achievement, and Rajveer could not hide his pleasure. With adrenalin rushing through him, he picked up his satellite phone and called the TIA chief. It was one in the morning.

'All well?' the TIA chief asked. He sounded alert and awake, as if he was expecting a call any time.

'Imran is with us,' Rajveer said.

'Don't knock him off,' the chief said. 'We need him here to expose the Pakistani conspiracy.'

'Copy that, sir,' Rajveer replied.

The team switched off all lights in the house and along the boundary wall and waited for Adnan bhai and his team. At around two o'clock, dogs started barking in the distance. The team readied their weapons and took cover from inside the boundary wall. Chacha opened the gate. He was clearly unarmed, and the team waited for him to enter. He knocked at the door of the house and, as ordered by Rajveer, Amjad opened it. As soon as Chacha walked in, he was taken down by the SSG. His wireless set was seized and he was asked to give them the code. It was 'Come for namaz'. Chacha revealed that Adnan bhai and the men with him were heavily armed.

Adnan and his group of four Lashkar-e-Jabbar cadres reached in the next ten minutes. Rajveer made a quick decision—which turned out to be the right one. He told the SSG team to take them on without first engaging in any verbal communication.

As soon as Adnan and his men spotted the SSG team, they opened fire and tried to escape. But Adnan did not stand a chance in the open fields, especially with trained SSG commandos well-positioned behind a solid cover. All five terrorists were killed.

Rajveer and his team asked Amjad to take out his pickup vehicle and put the dead bodies in it. Imran and Chacha were handcuffed and the team hurried away. It would not be long before the Nepali police arrived. Within twenty minutes of the operation, the team was headed towards the Sanauli border.

Rajveer called the TIA chief again. 'Mission accomplished,' he said. 'Five delta and three alpha.'

The chief was pleased. Five terrorists dead and three caught alive was news worth sharing with the Union security adviser.

'Sir, we need some help,' Rajveer said.

'Tell me,' the chief said, eager to assist in whatever way possible to ensure that Rajveer and his team reached the Indian side safely and quickly.

'Please pass on a message to the Defence Service Bureau guards (DSB) at the Sanauli border not to stop our convoy. We are in three civil vehicles and will reach in twenty minutes.'

'Done,' the chief replied. He had a big smile on his face, realizing how big an achievement it was.

When Rajveer and his team reached the Sanauli border after half an hour, the gates were open, as if the DSB was waiting for their return. No questions were asked.

The previous guard commander was conspicuously absent, a little embarrassed having realized who he had taken money from earlier.

After the three vehicles crossed the border to the Indian side, Rajveer could hear the sound of the gates being closed.

The Nepal police reached the scene of action at 3 a.m. By that time, there was no sign of anyone, and they could only find bloodstains in the nearby fields. The woman who had been in the house, the only eyewitness, had fled the spot, fearing for her life.

* * *

The interrogation of Chacha and Amjad revealed how deeply Pakistan was involved in fake Indian currency smuggling and in the infiltration of Lashkar-e-Jabbar cadres into India. A Pakistani passport and an embassy identity card were recovered from Chacha. His mobile phone was analysed by forensic experts, who recovered Google Chat data with the ISI. A total of around Rs 800 crore worth of fake Indian currency had been smuggled, and at least twenty groups of well-trained Pakistani Lashkar-e-Jabbar cadres had been facilitated.

Most importantly, the TIA found the evidence they had been looking for. The ISI and Chacha exchanged congratulatory messages at the time the attack was happening at Baramulla. Major Azim Afzal, Chacha's handler in Pakistan, praised the fidayeen action led by Abu Umer. They also discussed the *ghaibana namaz-e-jinaza* (the last namaz offered in absentia), to be performed at Shakargarh, and Major Afzal had assured that none other than Maulana Majid Asgar would be attending the final prayer in honour of Abu Umer.

The ISI shut down operations in Nepal owing to the huge embarrassment caused by Chacha's disclosures. A meeting was called at the Rawalpindi office of the ISI to discuss the issue. Maulana Asgar was invited as the guest of honour.

'We lost five brothers in Nepal,' Maulana Asgar said.

'Someone leaked the information,' Brig. Aslam said. 'We have to find out who. Ask Col. Yahya to carry out investigations and send a report.' Yahya was the military attaché at the Pakistani embassy in Nepal.

'Till the matter in Nepal is resolved, we will shift operations to the Indo–Bangladesh border,' Brig. Aslam said. Little did he realize that there was no human intelligence involved in the Nepal operation—it was all courtesy of the intercepted calls.

The TIA kept working on the Bangladeshi numbers and intercepted a vital communication that revealed that a group of Lashkar-e-Jabbar terrorists were going to infiltrate the country via Bangladesh. The group was caught in Malda in January 2015, and four terrorists were eliminated in the encounter. This time, Langda was among those killed.

Maulana Majid Asgar was distraught. He turned to Manzoor Trali, who was out of jail on bail. Trali was given charge of infiltrating Lashkar-e-Jabbar cadres from any possible route. Maulana Asgar also discussed the future course of action with Brig. Aslam. Clearly, the Bangladesh and Nepal channels had been exposed and had to be stopped forthwith, he said.

Brig. Aslam told him that there would be a meeting with Chinese army officials in Kabul after a few months, and invited Maulana Asgar to be a part of it. With their presence along the eastern border in Ladakh and along the Sikkim and Arunachal border, he was hopeful of getting a positive response from the Chinese to the problems of infiltration of the mujahideen into Jammu and Kashmir.

Maulana Asgar excused himself, citing the month of Ramadan as the reason. He would send his brother to attend the meeting instead, he said.

Chapter 8

It was a bright Sunday morning and Nikita, Aakriti and the grandparents were sitting on their lawn, enjoying the sunshine and playing a fun game of Ludo. Rajveer's parents had volunteered to come and stay with them for the initial months of the pregnancy so that Nikita could take care of herself while they enjoyed themselves taking care of Aakriti.

'I am the good one. I am Papa. I am going to kill all of you mean people and keep the place safe for the good ones,' Aakriti announced in a dramatic tone. Her grandparents were secretly happy to see ambition rising in the young child, but Nikita had mixed feelings. She was not sure if she wanted her daughter to walk the same path as her husband, though, of course, she was proud of her husband, without a fragment of doubt. Rajveer smiled at the innocence of his daughter.

Aakriti was strategizing with her grandfather. 'Dadaji, my tokens are red and yours are yellow. I promise not to cut any of yours. You promise not to cut any of mine. And let's together take away Ma's and Dadi's tokens.'

Rajveer began to think about how the terrorist organizations had begun using young boys as tokens in their game of Ludo.

* * *

'We must hit India with all our might,' Brig. Aslam had said. Maulana agreed. He had lost nine hardcore cadres of the Lashkar-e-Jabbar recently.

The war room of the Lashkar-e-Jabbar in Bahawalpur was packed for the repeat *namaz-e-jinaza* of the *shaheed*, martyrs as the Lashkar-e-Jabbar called them. The grieving congregation was consoled by Maulana Asgar, who promised revenge. 'The Indian security forces will have to pay for this,' he said. 'Adnan bhai was my nephew and barely twenty-five years old. *Allah unki shahadat qabool farmaye aur unko jannat ata farmaye.* (May Allah accept his martyrdom and place him in heaven.)'

Maulana appealed to those assembled to volunteer for a special mission they had planned for the first day of 2016. 'The plan is big,' he said. 'We need volunteers who will follow the path of Allah and are willing to sacrifice their lives in the name of jihad. Maulana Zaif will interview volunteers to assess your suitability after the namaz,' he said.

Maulana Zaif roped in ARQ to help him interview volunteers. No one knew the ground requirements in Kashmir better than ARQ.

The interviews were meant to assess the volunteer's understanding of jihad in the manner taught by the Lashkar-e-Jabbar, their commitment towards jihad, their physical fitness, their daily commitment to perform namaz as per

Islamic practices and their sense of discipline. Maulana
Zaif was of the firm view that, to become a suicide attacker,
one needed to be very disciplined.

The interviews were completed by the evening and
four people were chosen among the scores of volunteers:
Nasir Shafi, Abu Bakar Siddiqui, Umar Malik and Abdul
Qayum. Kashif Mohammed and Rashid Latif were given
charge of training the four men.

The Lashkar-e-Jabbar was determined to carry out their
plan as soon as possible, so the training began immediately.

All six were taken to a room. There, on one wall, was a
screen on which was displayed a Google map of India.

Maulana Zaif took charge and explained the plan.

'The air force station at Gurdaspur in India is the
closest military airport to the Pakistan border. To make
things easier, our Lashkar-e-Jabbar launching headquarters
is at Shakargarh, not very far away from the Gurdaspur
border. We have already spoken to the ISI at the military
cantonment at Bahawalpur, and they have assured full
support to our mujahid,' Maulana Zaif said. 'Our plan
is to carry out a fidayeen attack on 1 January at the air
force station at Gurdaspur—one that will cause as many
casualties as possible. We will try to destroy the military
planes and their missile depot. One group of two mujahids
should try to move towards the family quarters as soon as
you enter the air force station, while the other group will
try to hijack a vehicle from inside and travel towards the
technical area of the air force station.'

Pointing to the screen, on which the Gurdaspur air force
station was now being displayed, Maulana Zaif continued.
'The air force station is spread over a massive area and

the boundary wall is almost 15 km long. The guards are positioned all along the wall. You can see the dense forest area, behind which there are hangars for the planes and a missile unit. Do not target these areas immediately as they are well guarded. Do you see this small clean patch on the screen?'

'Yes,' everyone replied in unison.

'This is a *ziarat* (shrine),' Zaif said. 'A man called Hafiz Aleem oversees the holy tomb, and there is a congregation here every Thursday. Hafiz will be your guide after you get into the air force station.'

The briefing continued till late in the night, after which the six selected men dispersed. Before they left, the maulana looked them in the eye and said, 'You have one chance to meet your families before you walk on the path of Allah. A vehicle and a driver are at your disposal and will take you wherever you want.' The Lashkar-e-Jabbar always made sure that new recruits were taken good care of, so they would want to continue with the organization and would believe that their families would be looked after even if they were no longer around.

One of the men, Nasir Shafi, asked his driver, Shahid bhai, to head towards his ancestral village at Vihari. The Toyota pickup vehicle—a favourite among mujahids— turned off the main road and drove down a kutcha track for 2 km. They stopped at a dead end and both got down. They crossed a small river on foot and reached the house where Nasir's mother Rizwana, brother Mudasir, wife Sakeena and six-year-old son Altamash were awaiting his return.

'Where have you been?' Rizwana asked with concern. 'Who is with you?' she continued in a whisper. They were not used to guests coming to their humble abode. They had barely enough to feed themselves.

'He is Shahid bhai,' Nasir replied, a little embarrassed at his mother's directness.

After a few pleasantries and a general exchange of information on his whereabouts, Nasir took his wife aside, telling her he wanted to discuss something important with her. Sakeena, a simple and submissive lady, immediately sat down to listen to her husband.

'I will be going away for a few weeks,' Nasir said. 'There is a job offer that I have to take to make your lives comfortable. Inshallah, you will have enough money to take care of yourselves. It will almost be like a lifelong pension for us.' Nasir knew that the Lashkar-e-Jabbar had a well-established system of taking care of anyone who committed himself to the cause of jihad.

'Where do you have to go to take up this job? Will you be able to visit us after a few weeks? Is it not possible for you to take me and Altamash along?' Sakeena asked.

'The work is near Shakargarh. Let me reach there once and assess the conditions. Then I can figure out the future course of action,' Nasir lied, hoping it would be enough to pacify his wife.

When Sakeena seemed convinced, Nasir headed out of his home to look for the man he had always looked up to, Ustaad. He owed all his skills in carpentry to the Ustaad, and would never do anything without taking him into confidence. A man with a long beard, Ustaad was a devout Muslim and offered namaz five times a day without fail. Nasir decided to share the truth with Ustaad. He told him about his meeting with Maulana Majid Asgar, and the fact that they had chosen him for a special mission. He did not disclose the exact plan but conveyed that it could cost him his life. Ustaad listened to Nasir with an expressionless face. He was himself a committed maulvi. Once, he had visited Bahawalpur to listen to Maulana Asgar speak and had been very impressed with the clarity of thought. Had he not been old, he would have volunteered for jihad himself.

'You have to do me a favour,' Nasir said. 'Prepare a will entrusting all my property to Sakeena and Altamash. Also, convince Mudasir to marry Sakeena in case I do not return.'

When Ustaad had agreed, Nasir returned home. He was determined to create some happy memories with his family with the time remaining. He took his wife and son to Multan, and bought Altamash 'angreji khilone', as they called toys from the West. Sakeena was surprised at her husband's generosity, and she herself received an expensive salwar kameez. They also picked up some clothes for Rizwana. It felt like Eid.

As they headed back home, Sakeena—who never questioned Nasir—said, 'Looks like you finally have a decent job offer ...' She hoped he would volunteer information on what kind of job he had. But Nasir only smiled and looked down at his son.

Finally, he said, 'Yes, at least it's one that can give my mother, brother, you and Altamash financial security.' His wife noticed that he had not included his own name among the beneficiaries.

The next morning, he visited the bank and made his account a joint one with his wife. He handed over to her important documents, including that of his ancestral land—for safe custody, he said. Having tied up all the loose ends, he packed a bag with some essentials and told Shahid bhai he was ready to leave. At the door, he picked up Altamash and kissed his forehead. '*Khuda hafiz*,' he said to his family and then left.

Nasir reached Bahawalpur the next day, where the rest of the team was waiting for him. Two Toyota cars were standing at the ready. Rashid Latif, Umar and Qayum climbed into one, and Kashif, Abu Bakar and Nasir got into the other. Thus began their 600-km journey to the border town of Shakargarh via Multan and Lahore. They stopped for dinner in Lahore, offered the evening namaz at the famous Badshahi mosque, and then continued on, finally reaching the Lashkar-e-Jabbar camp at Shakargarh at midnight.

Earlier a part of Sialkot district, Shakargarh was now in the newly formed Narowal district of Pakistan. Before Partition, it was a tehsil of Gurdaspur district and thus not far from Gurdaspur as the crow flies across the border between India and Pakistan. Besides the Ravi River, which divided the town into two, the only known places in Shakargarh were the ISI Dett (detachment) and the Lashkar-e-Jabbar camp, which was not very far away from the ISI Dett. Rashid Latif had served in this Lashkar-e-Jabbar camp for five years as the head of the camp responsible for training and launching Lashkar-e-Jabbar cadres.

The attack team hit their beds straight after reaching, having travelled almost ten hours by road. Early next morning, after namaz, Rashid took them to the war room of the Lashkar-e-Jabbar, which had stocks of arms and ammunition, grenades, wireless sets, IED material, dry rations to survive a gunfight for at least forty-eight hours,

SOS medicines and injections to suppress any kind of pain (even one from a bullet injury), GPS equipment, diver suits and waterproof carry bags.

Abu Bakar picked up an AK-47 rifle and admired the finish on the woodwork. The excitement of the men on seeing brand new equipment was no less than that of children when they receive a fresh set of books for a new school session.

Kashif then took them to the Ravi River and they were given basic training in swimming just below the surface of the water with the help of a snorkel. 'You would have done something like this in the sea while training at the Karachi camp,' Kashif said. The men had heard about similar training given to Lashkar-e-Taiba mujahids by someone known as the 'Frog Man'. They did not know his real name but knew he was a retired navy officer who had trained the terrorists in the Mumbai attack.

The intensive training was repeated over the next three days. On the fourth day, Rashid explained the plan.

'You, Nasir, Umar, Abu Bakar and Qayum, will be dropped at the border at Bamiyal. From there, you have to enter India along the riverbed. The only place where there is no fence is along the water flow line. You'll have to wear your diver suits and swim across the section where the river takes a U-turn and the water current is towards India,' Rashid said.

Kashif took out the lunar calendar and said, 'According to this calendar, it gets completely dark after eight o'clock at night. This is the right time for you to get by, avoiding the eyes of the BSF.'

The river near the Bamiyal border meandered and took a U-turn once it entered Pakistan from the Indian side. It then again meandered back towards Pakistan. This made swimming across to the Indian side easier. The BSF had made an improvised fence on the river with floating concertina wires. Although it prevented anyone from swimming across, anyone using a snorkel could cross the floating fence and exit behind the BSF deployment.

The mujahids readied themselves with their backpacks and headed to the Bamiyal border with Kashif and Rashid. There, they waited for the sun to set. As soon as the clock struck eight, Rashid and Kashif bid them goodbye. They hugged each other, saying what all mujahids do before embarking on any mission, '*Naara-e-Taqbeer, Allah-o-Akbar.*'

* * *

The water was freezing cold. They put on their diving suits, ensured that their backpacks were firmly attached, and then, one by one, they entered the water, maintaining a minute gap between each of them. They swam for about 200 metres and then reached the other bank. Nasir was the first one to get to the bank and waited there for the others to join him. They looked back and could see the BSF post, with searchlights aimed towards the international border, looking for suspicious movement on the Pakistani side. Little did they realize that four mujahids, using the meandering river, had exited towards the rear of the BSF camp.

Nasir and his group pulled off their diving suits and changed into their kurtas. They threw away their wet shoes and put on the new Woodland shoes given to them by the Lashkar-e-Jabbar at Shakargarh. They walked a kilometre along the river with the help of a Garmin GPS device, till they finally hit the roadhead. The GPS device showed the Gurdaspur Airbase was 30 km away.

They waited there for any vehicle moving in the direction they needed to go. It was ten o'clock.

Chapter 9

Ujagar Singh, a local taxi driver, was returning from a visit to his newfound love at Bamiyal. He would visit her clandestinely, after everyone in the village fell asleep, and was now returning with a whisky quarter in his hand, enjoying the latest Punjabi romantic number on his car stereo.

Suddenly, four men stepped forward on to the road, and Ujagar Singh quickly pressed down on the brake. He had never seen anyone at this remote place so late in the night. The car screeched to a halt. All four men got into the car before he could say anything. Nasir got into the front seat and pointed his pistol at Ujagar.

'Take us to the Gurdaspur Airbase,' Nasir said.

Ujagar had barely finished one-third of the liquor bottle and was still in his senses. 'This is trouble,' he said to himself. The days of militancy in Punjab had got over long ago, and people were now used to a peaceful life. Anyway, the men were not wearing turbans and were clearly not Sikhs. He tried to start a conversation: 'Where are you coming from?' he asked.

'Keep driving. That's none of your business,' replied Nasir.

Ujagar shut up. '*Jaan hai to jahan hai* (One can enjoy the world only if one is alive),' he thought.

Nasir began talking to the others in Punjabi. '*Asi blue line ch follow karange* (We will follow this blue line),' he said, pointing out the blue line showing the canal on the GPS map.

Realizing that the Punjabi dialect was from the Pakistani side of Punjab, Ujagar became alert. He was now sure that something major was going to happen. 'A terror attack,' he said to himself. He was a righteous man and a pure Khalsa. 'Time to save lives,' he said to himself. He twisted the wheel of his car, taking the vehicle down the side of a road where it crashed into the trunk of a tree.

The car was damaged, and the parking lights started flashing. Ujagar jumped out of the car and tried to run away. Nasir ran behind him and got hold of him. He took out his knife and slit the driver's throat. Ujagar fell to the ground, blood oozing out of his throat. He shook for some time before he finally stopped breathing.

'He was a *kafir* (infidel),' Nasir said.

The mujahid switched off the car's engine, so the parking lights would stop blinking and then turned it on again. They then drove the damaged vehicle for some distance before leaving it at an isolated place and waited for another car.

Soon enough, one came along with two men in it.

* * *

Shaitan Singh had recently been transferred from the post of executive engineer in Gurdaspur and had complained about it to his cook, Ajit. The position had been a lucrative one and clearly, if he lost money, the cook would also lose out, since he would no longer get generous freebies from his employer. Ajit had suggested that they go to a baba who would put an end to their problems. 'The baba is powerful and can tell you ways to help you keep the original posting,' he said. So, they proceeded to the baba's ashram and met him late at night.

The baba had offered them tea, after which he took them to his meditation room where there were different types of stones arranged in concentric circles. In the middle was a small carpet, and the baba sat down on it. Shaitan Singh and Ajit were made to sit in one corner of the room. The baba then lit his hookah and, after smoking five rounds, he went into a trance and began talking to spirits. The conversation was in a language that Shaitan and Ajit could not understand. It ended after ten minutes. Baba opened his eyes and gave them a note scribbled on a piece of paper. 'Keep this under your pillow for three days,' he said. 'You should not open the paper and see what is written inside. It's meant only for the higher spirits to see.'

Happy that the baba had promised an immediate remedy, Shaitan Singh was now returning from the ashram via Bamiyal, his cook in the front seat beside him.

Suddenly, their car was stopped by a few men.

* * *

The mujahids stopped the vehicle and asked them to get down. Having learnt their lesson from the previous attempt to hijack a car, this time, Nasir took the driver's seat. Both Shaitan Singh and his cook were pinned down in the backseat, with Umar and Qayum sitting on top of them. Abu Bakar sat beside Nasir and gave him directions to the Gurdaspur Airbase. As they drove quickly down the roads, Nasir told the other mujahids to take Shaitan Singh's phone from him and told him to unlock it. Once unlocked, they made a call to Maulana Zaif, assuming that making a short call from the phone of a local would cause no harm and could not be traced.

Maulana Zaif picked up immediately. He was not expecting a call at this time. Making a phone call was not as per the usual standard operating procedure (SOP) of the mujahids. 'We are on our way and all is well,' Nasir said.

'Okay, switch off the phone and no further calls till you achieve the task Allah has bestowed upon you,' Maulana Zaif said.

'*Ithe hara koi gyani hai*,' Nasir said to his fellow mujahids—it is easier to preach than follow. Ignoring the maulana's instructions, he then made a call to Ustaad.

'We're on our mission and will be successful, Inshallah,' he said when Ustaad picked up.

'May Allah give you the strength to be successful,' Ustaad replied.

They approached a thick, forested area, and the mujahid dumped Shaitan Singh and his cook there, their hands tied. 'Don't move from here till it is first light,' Nasir said.

They drove on, following the canal, and reached the boundary wall of the Gurdaspur Airbase at around four o'clock, when it was still dark. Hafiz Aleem, the man who was in charge of the nearby *ziarat*, had sent Rashid Latif the GPS coordinates of the best point at which to scale the wall, and those had already been fed into the GPS.

They abandoned the car close to the bushes along the canal, making sure that it was not visible from a distance. They then crossed the canal, which had very little water, and then walked towards the airbase wall. It was absolutely still. The air force staff, except those on sentry duty, had slept late after the New Year's party and were now in deep sleep.

Nasir and the others pulled out the rope ladders from their backpacks, donned their night vision glasses and began scaling the wall at the predetermined point.

Once inside the station, they followed the route given by Hafiz Aleem to reach an abandoned store near the MT fleet of the station. They had been told to remain there for an hour and carry out the attack just before first light. Nasir then called his mother.

'We have started on the path of Allah. Please take care of Sakeena and Altamash,' he said.

Sensing what Nasir was hinting at, Rizwana maintained her calm. 'Take care of yourself. You are like a lion—nothing is going to happen to you,' his mother said, trying to instil confidence in him. 'Allah *hafiz*.'

While the mujahids were hiding in the abandoned store, a routine drone sortie looking for any suspicious behaviour hovered around the international border and then turned back towards the Gurdaspur Airbase.

'Sir, there is something unusual at the storehouse,' Ranjana Mathur, the chief flight controller told the air officer commanding, Prateek Mishra, on the phone.

It was four-thirty in the morning, and the AOC was clearly unhappy with the early morning wake-up call. 'What is it?' he asked.

'Sir, footage at the control room is showing four dots moving in an unusual manner at the storehouse. More importantly, no one stays there,' she said.

This is alarming, the AOC thought to himself. Movement at this hour and at that location in the airbase was very unusual. He was now completely awake and immediately called for an alert at the airbase. The sirens went off and all the staff at the airbase assembled, including the Garud Commandos. Wing Commander Ashish Sood, the chief of the Garud Commandos, was asked to immediately cordon off the storehouse.

While the cordon was being put in place, the AOC hurriedly addressed his men, taking care not to create panic. The aircraft at the airbase were given additional security cover and all vital installations were doubly secured.

The AOC then headed to the air traffic control unit and began watching the drone footage. The thermal indicators were clear: there were four dots together in the storehouse. The AOC could now also see, through the hot flashes of light on the screen, that the cordon was being laid.

Suddenly, the AOC said, 'Hell, firing has started at the storehouse!' He grabbed his walkie-talkie and shouted, 'Tiger 2, this is Tiger 1, do you hear me?'

'Copy that, sir,' Ashish replied.

'What's happening there?' the AOC asked.

Ashish replied hurriedly, 'One Golf Charlie down, firefight started. Over.'

'Shit! We have one Garud Commando down,' the AOC told the officers around him.

Huge flashes were now visible at the MT fleet. Some parked vehicles had caught fire during the gunfight.

Despite the casualty, the situation was under control, the AOC thought. The terrorists, clearly heavily armed, were confined to one location, and all the vital installations and aircraft had been secured.

But then two of the terrorists took advantage of a gap in the cordon and snuck out to the cookhouse, firing indiscriminately. Three more air force personnel were injured. One of the cooks, Pehalwan Singh, had gone to the washroom and was on his way back when he heard firing. He was an international wrestler and, without any fear for his own life, he caught hold of one of the terrorists from behind. The rifle held by the terrorist was snatched and thrown away. While they got into a physical fight, Pehalwan Singh reached out for a knife in the room and slit the terrorist's throat. The other terrorist there had held his fire while this was going on. When he saw his associate fall to the ground, he fired at Pehalwan Singh, killing the brave soldier.

Bulletproof vehicles were pressed into service and the men in them engaged the remaining terrorists. After three hours of firefighting, all the terrorists were killed and four air force personnel were martyred.

The AOC called Ashish to his room after the encounter was over. 'I am proud of you, Ashish,' he said. 'Sorry for the loss of our boys.'

Ashish acknowledged the AOC's words and then said, 'Sir, the TIA is sending a team on a special flight today. It will be led by IG Rajveer Singh.'

The AOC nodded. 'Send a team to receive them and one to secure the encounter site till they collect evidence.'

* * *

Rajveer got down from the aircraft with his team of fifteen experts, which included a forensic team. They divided the scene of action into three sections, and an officer of Dy SP rank was given charge of each. Rajveer briefed his men before the search began.

'Scan your respective areas minutely and collect every possible piece of evidence. The idea is simple. We have to establish four things. Firstly, that a terrorist act has taken place. Secondly, the attackers were terrorists. Thirdly and importantly, if there are any links to Pakistan. And, finally, is there any link between these attackers, the killing of a man, and the abduction of two other men last night.'

The TIA team got working right away. It started a grid search of the area, collecting each piece of evidence. They took the help of the bomb disposal squad to destroy all unexploded grenades and rockets. The bodies of the terrorists were photographed, and DNA evidence was collected and preserved. Rajveer noticed that the attackers were all clean-shaven—typical of suicide attackers. A mobile phone was found with one of the terrorists, and that was taken away to be analysed.

The backpacks were searched and the contents were examined.

'This is interesting,' Rajveer said to the AOC, who was accompanying him. 'The dry fruit packets are half full and have the label "Altaf Store, Shakargarh, Pakistan". How far is Shakargarh from here?'

'It's 45 kilometres as the crow flies,' replied the AOC. 'Around 10 kilometres from the international border.'

A milk cream packet with the terrorists carried the label 'Nestle Milk Pak Cream', manufactured by Nestle Pakistan

Ltd, 308, Upper Mall, Lahore, and the SOS injections were made by GlaxoSmithKline Pakistan.

'Three things are clear so far from the evidence,' Rajveer told the AOC. 'That the attackers were Pakistanis, that they came from the Shakargarh border side, and that they were all suicide attackers.'

Once the call history on the mobile phone was checked, the Pakistani connection to the attackers became even more clear. One of the phone numbers contacted was the same as one prominently flashed on an advertisement for the Al Khidmat Trust. The trust, they knew, was run by the Lashkar-e-Jabbar as a front.

Rajveer headed back to New Delhi, leaving the team behind to continue with the investigations. He had been summoned to the chamber of the Union security adviser where he was asked for a detailed update.

'Sir, there appears to be good evidence that the Lashkar-e-Jabbar was involved,' Rajveer said. 'Also, all the attackers are Pakistanis.'

'Any evidence that Maulana Majid Asgar was involved?' the Union security adviser asked.

'Sir, we have very good evidence against his brother Maulana Zaif Asgar,' Rajveer said. 'Fortunately for us, the executive engineer's phone, which the terrorists seized and used, had phone call recording activated. So, all their conversations are recorded on the phone and can be easily retrieved forensically.

'There is good evidence against Maulana Majid Asgar too,' Rajveer continued. 'When the encounter was going on, Maulana Asgar sent out an audio message on their Facebook page, praising the act of his mujahids.

The Facebook account can easily be verified and connected to Maulana Asgar. In the message, he mentioned the names of Umar, Nasir, Abu Bakar and Qayum. On the call recordings, we heard Nasir's name being taken by two of the people the terrorist spoke to. So there is that link between Maulana Asgar and the attackers.'

'Excellent work,' the Union security adviser said. 'You deserve a medal for this investigation! Try and finish it soon and present a chargesheet indicting Maulana Asgar and Zaif as accused.'

Rajveer felt a sense of contentment on being recognized for his work but was also immediately reminded of the conversation he happened to hear in the steam bath years ago. But that was the way it was, he knew. Sometimes, operations were successful and the officer was lauded; sometimes they were not, and the officer was criticized. Yet, in both, the officer would have been just as earnest and hardworking. He shrugged. He had work to do!

The investigations went on for three months, after which a charge sheet was filed against eight accused, including Maulana Asgar, Maulana Zaif, Rashid Latif, Kashif and the four attackers. A Red Corner notice—an Interpol notice for the arrest of absconding accused—was issued against all those based in Pakistan. With the new evidence that the Al Khidmat Trust and the Lashkar-e-Jabbar were linked, the investigation was also now able to pin down the trust for terror financing.

Owing to international pressure from all sides, Pakistan had no choice but to constitute a team to look into the evidence. They were also under pressure to take action against the Al Khidmat Trust. India, meanwhile, pressed for proscribing Maulana Asgar and Maulana Zaif as international terrorists.

Pakistan now looked toward its old ally, China, to protect the monster that was their own brainchild. When the proposal came up for voting, China voted against proscribing Maulana Asgar and Maulana Zaif as international terrorists. The Union security adviser of India pressed diplomatic efforts with the country's allies, the Americans, British and French, to support its cause of curbing terrorism and terror financing. Finally, unable to evade the pressure created by overwhelming evidence presented by the TIA, the Chinese relented and Maulana Agar and Maulana Zaif were finally declared international terrorists.

It was a victory for India and another nail in the coffin for the Lashkar-e-Jabbar. Or was it the curse of the pir?!

Chapter 10

The year was going to be a busy one for Rajveer on the personal front. His brother Suresh was getting married, after which he and his wife would be moving abroad; Payal—Nikita's sister—was also going abroad for a three-year course; and, of course, his and Nikita's second child was due soon. It was a busy year for him professionally, too. He still had two years of his deputation period left with the TIA, but he wanted to be where the action was. Torn between wanting to be with his family and being where he would get true professional satisfaction, he brought up the topic with Nikita. Once again, she stated what a true-blooded Indian would, saying: 'Go where you are needed more. These are your days to work and reach professional heights. Be where you will be satisfied professionally.' Rajveer was reminded of how lucky he was to have married her. He gave it some more thought and finally decided to return to Jammu and Kashmir.

Since so much was happening in the family, Rajveer invited both his and Nikita's families to celebrate Holi with them at their Delhi residence, before they all headed in their own directions. The day before Holi, when everyone was at home, having a good laugh and enjoying time together, Nikita felt a cramp. Three hours later, they were all at the hospital, waiting outside the operating theatre. The baby had decided to join the family for Holi, Rajveer thought happily.

'It's a boy!' the doctor announced. Being the time of mobile phones, quick pictures were taken and shared on the family group. Immediate congratulatory notes appeared, along with keen observations such as, 'He looks like Rajveer', 'His nose is exactly like his grandfather's', 'He is a duplicate of Aakriti'. They decided to name the boy Niraj, as it had a bit of both Nikita and Rajveer.

A week later, Rajveer headed back to Jammu and Kashmir, leaving behind his family in Delhi. Considering his experience with investigations, he was immediately asked to head the Crime Branch.

Rajveer's office was in Jehangir Chowk, overlooking the huge secretariat building, the seat of power in Jammu and Kashmir. Jehangir Chowk's claim to fame was not just that it had the secretariat building—this was also the place where the Lashkar-e-Jabbar carried out their first deadly attack after their formation in 2001. They placed a Tata Sumo in the chowk outside the Assembly and caused it to explode, killing seven innocent civilians. They then stormed the Assembly complex, where they could not do much damage before they were gunned down.

'Interestingly,' thought Rajveer, 'in both their attempts to target temples of democracy—one at the Legislative Assembly in Srinagar and the other in the Parliament in Delhi—they were unable to kill a single politician.'

Rajveer immediately got on to his daily regime of going to the gym, following it up with a steam bath, returning home, reading the newspaper with his breakfast, and then heading to work. In the office, in order to maintain a certain discipline and manage all his work, he designed a schedule for himself which he shared with his personal staff the very first day, and they were quick to adapt. This is how his day would be, he told them. 'I would like to keep the first few hours of the day for important meetings,' he said, adding with a smile, 'because I am fresh and my mind functions better then. Following that, some time should be kept for staff meetings where they can come to discuss issues related to their work or even personal issues that are bothering them. Finally, we must keep some time for politicians and media personnel who may want to visit.'

He knew well that he was in a sensitive post, and was likely to have politicians and media inviting themselves to his office. He wanted to keep them all in good humour. 'Adjust the politicians and media personnel keeping in mind my scheduled meetings.'

Even as he was speaking, he was thinking, 'There will always be time for lunches with colleagues where assignments are informally discussed and, more importantly, where I can get news from the grapevine.'

He was not one to waste time, and on his second day in office, he called for the investigation files on the Lashkar-e-Jabbar. He began chatting with his staff officer, Mushtaq Zari.

'Tell me about the parole case of Manzoor Trali,' he asked Mushtaq.

'Sir, it's very strange that he got bail, considering his deep and established involvement with the Lashkar-e-Jabbar and arms smuggling,' Mushtaq said.

'So, he is still out on good behaviour? Do we have any idea what he's been up to and if he's engaging in terrorist activities? Does anyone review these cases?' Rajveer asked.

Mushtaq requested that he be given some time to ask around. 'There is no SOP here to monitor each parole case. The cases are supposed to be monitored by the local station house officer (SHO),' he said.

* * *

Since the day Manzoor Trali had come out on parole, he had been largely based in and around Tral. The Lashkar-e-Jabbar kept him confined to south Kashmir, which was their stronghold. They wanted their most trusted man there to facilitate and coordinate their activities. To be on parole and to keep working for the Lashkar-e-Jabbar, Manzoor Trali cultivated men among the lower subordinates at each important branch of the state police. Basharat Khan, a resident of Pampore working as a clerk at the Crime Branch, was the first one to send a message to Ashqoor, Manzoor Trali's elder brother.

'The new IG of the Crime Branch was asking about you,' Ashqoor told his brother.

'Is he the same one who was heading the Gurdaspur investigations?' Manzoor Trali asked.

Ashqoor shook his head. 'I have no idea about that,' he replied.

Manzoor Trali decided to make a trip to the Crime Branch office in his run-down 'Marwati'—the name Kashmiris give the Maruti Suzuki car. With the seat almost touching the steering wheel because of his height, he headed out from his village and then hit the main road at Awantipora. He took a right turn and drove towards

Pantha Chowk. He passed the Badami Bagh cantonment, thinking of the days when they had exploded a Marwati laden with explosives outside the main gate. As he drove past, he looked right and said a prayer for the departed mujahid. '*Allaahum-maghfirlahu Allaahum-mathabbithu.*' [O Allah, forgive him. O Allah, strengthen him.]

After ninety minutes of driving, Manzoor reached the Jehangir Chowk flyover from where he looked at the Crime Branch headquarters. 'Had it been ten years ago, we could have bombed this office,' he told himself.

Today, he was in a conciliatory mood. He had a family to sustain and had been in jail for a very long time. More importantly, he had found the equilibrium of sustaining the activities of Lashkar-e-Jabbar from the backseat, while fulfilling the conditions of the parole. He was in no mood to pick up the gun himself again.

***

'Sir, a person by the name of Manzoor has come to meet you,' an orderly said to Rajveer.

'Bring him in,' said Rajveer, looking up from his papers.

Rajveer had never seen Manzoor Trali before, but the man who walked in was so short, Rajveer could make an intelligent guess that this was the well-known terrorist. Offering him a seat, Rajveer studied Manzoor, particularly his body language and his eye movements. The terrorist was not meeting Rajveer's eyes, but his body posture projected composure.

'What are you doing these days?' asked Rajveer, once Manzoor had sat down.

'Nothing, except looking after my orchards and bringing up my children,' Manzoor said.

'When does your parole period expire?'

'Sir, I have two more weeks, but it should be extended as per past practice, as long as I have your blessings,' Manzoor said, adding, 'The judge has been kind and I have left the path of violence.'

Rajveer, who had trained with the FBI and had done the National Academy Graduates Programme with them, used the tricks learnt there. The lessons came back in a flash to him and he remembered what he had learnt about face reading and statement analysis. In fact, in those seconds, he remembered a Pakistani counterpart, Asif Qureshi, who was also doing the programme with him, who was from the infamous Abbottabad. Qureshi had been constantly quizzed about how Osama bin Laden managed to stay so close to the army cantonment. He appeared completely ignorant of how this would have been possible. Later, when Rajveer and the instructor, Albert Callaghar, were having a cup of coffee together, Callaghar had explained in detail, based on facial expressions and the inconsistency of his statements, how and why he thought that Qureshi was not being truthful.

Now, Rajveer looked Manzoor straight in the eyes and said, 'No. You have been a part of the core team of the Lashkar-e-Jabbar and we know for sure that you are still in touch with the chief of the Lashkar-e-Jabbar.'

Manzoor was taken aback by the confidence with which Rajveer had said this. *What did the IG know*, he wondered.

In fact, Rajveer had no certain knowledge that Manzoor was still involved in terrorist activities, but something about the man had given him a strong sense that this was the case. He had decided to take a chance and make a direct accusation. Manzoor was definitely avoiding eye contact, which fuelled Rajveer's suspicions even more.

Manzoor was an established player himself though, and he kept quiet for some time. He weighed his options. Either he would be heading back to jail, or he could offer the IG a deal. He made his choice.

'Yes,' he said finally. 'I am in touch with Maulana Asgar,' he said.

Rajveer's face did not show his jubilation. He had not expected to strike gold so easily.

'He talks to me when support is required for the mujahideen,' Manzoor said and continued. 'I organize protests against security forces whenever he tells me. Many times it is to help and facilitate the mujahideen to escape while the security forces grapple with the law and order situation.'

Manzoor cleverly avoided revealing that he had any direct knowledge of the presence of terrorists. He knew that if he disclosed all the details of his connections with the Lashkar-e-Jabbar, he would be sent back to prison immediately. Taking into account the IG's reputation, he assumed he would be sent to solitary confinement, which would put a stop to all the support he provided to the Lashkar-e-Jabbar. He was a launching commander, an overground worker, a preacher, a planner and a motivator— an all-in-one package for the Lashkar-e-Jabbar. Confident of his network in the security set-up and legal support from the Lashkar-e-Jabbar, he had not put in place a successor, someone who would be able to take over if he were not around.

Manzoor knew that he could dodge Rajveer a few times but, sooner or later, his activities would come under the scanner. He was aware that, as a mujahid, he had a limited life. Considering the average lifespan of a mujahid or an overground worker, Manzoor was possibly one of the longest-surviving ones. He decided to buy some time till he could identify a successor.

'Maulana Zaif is going to Afghanistan to meet Chinese authorities,' Manzoor said, confident that the information was good enough to buy him time, but it would also be of no use to Rajveer.

'What is he going there for?' asked Rajveer, keeping his gaze steady.

'Just a courtesy visit to thank them for their support to Maulana Asgar during tough times,' Manzoor said nonchalantly. 'The Chinese have also offered a permanent solution for the problems involved in sending in mujahideen through the LOC into Jammu and Kashmir. The visit is being coordinated by the ISI, and it will take place at Kunduz, where the Taliban will provide logistics.'

Rajveer remained expressionless, but he was excited to hear this. Having served with the central agencies, Rajveer had a wider perspective of looking at things. He knew that putting Trali in prison would not fetch him the best results. The activities of the Lashkar-e-Jabbar would no doubt get curbed, but it would be just a matter of time before they found a replacement for him and started their operations again. Tightening the screws on Trali, putting pressure on his contacts and family would also at best fetch him one or two successful operations leading to the elimination of some Lashkar-e-Jabbar terrorists. He decided the best option would be to let Trali be and keep a tighter vigil on him, while also working on the information he has just been gifted. His aim was to go to the depth of the activities of the Lashkar-e-Jabbar and get insights into their plans.

'Keep me informed of developments,' Rajveer said authoritatively. 'Remember, you're under watch, and any move or contact with Lashkar-e-Jabbar operatives will land you back in prison.'

Manzoor nodded. He was happy with the way the meeting had gone. He had not given away much and was now being let off. He had not expected this, especially after providing information which he thought would be of no use to Rajveer because it was practically useless. He knew that, for the Indian police, investigating any information based in Afghanistan was almost impossible.

Rajveer, on the other hand, was thinking big. He wanted to infiltrate the Lashkar-e-Jabbar system and have permanent assets who could provide them with vital inside information. Maneesh Mathur, his childhood friend and a pilot with Ariana Afghan Airlines, was the name that immediately flashed in his mind. He sent an invite to Maneesh to visit Kashmir on an all-paid visit.

While he had a leisurely lunch, his mind was on the way forward. He decided to summon the senior superintendent of police (SSP) to discuss the next course of action. SSP Mehak was someone he would see in his gym. She had caught his eye the first time he'd seen her, and he could see that she caught the eye of a lot of people. True to her name, she exuded a certain vibe, and the image of Mehak running on the treadmill had stayed in his mind for a while.

Now, he heard a soft knock on the door and Mehak entered the room. She took permission and then sat down in the chair in front of him. He wondered if she knew how attractive she was.

'Trali has given us a lead, and we need to start working on it,' he said, hoping to get an excited and positive response from Mehak.

'Sir, my experience with this kind of people has been that they purposely give wrong information in order to engage us in other matters while they carry on with their own stuff. This Trali chap is not to be trusted. He is one of the hardcore ones.'

Rajveer shook his head. 'I could tell he was being truthful. Also, he knows the consequences of lying to us. I don't think he would be willing to risk it.'

'Maybe not, sir. But I have met some very good resources and some extremely smart goons like Trali, thus my reaction. I personally feel we should take this with a pinch of salt.'

Rajveer was always one ready to hear stories about resources and learn from the experiences of his fellow officers. Though the matter did not quite deal with the issue at hand, he encouraged Mehak to tell him more about the resources. As his team member, he wanted her to be on the same page as him with respect to Trali, and at the same time, he wanted to engage her in conversation.

'Sir, like all officers, I have met resources who claim that they are on our side and give some inconsequential information in exchange for money. I am pretty certain that they are resources on the other side too. But I have had a very good resource who gave us information about ten terrorists. He said that he can give us the exact details of their hideout, and we could get all ten of them in one go.'

Rajveer was impressed. 'Did you really get all ten?'

'Yes, sir.'

'But this is not an easy job. Even if you do get to know about their hideouts, this being a hilly area, they can make a quick getaway and usually we're able to capture only a few.'

'Sir, this was a unique case. This resource had a personal axe to grind with the terrorists. A carpenter by profession, he was used to make concealed cupboards and floor boxes in which terrorists could rest. His services were used earlier also, and his work was so good, it was absolutely impossible to find these secret places even if one was told about them.'

'So, how come he changed loyalties and sided with you guys?'

'As I said, he had a personal axe to grind. He had an exceptionally beautiful sister and these extremists were harassing her. He felt the only way to get all of them out of his way was through us. But, I must admit, Sir, the guy's work was actually brilliant. He gave us exact details, drew the designs on paper and explained precisely how the concealed spaces could be reached. He was so done with the terrorists and their behaviour with his sister that he actually told us the number of grenades we should use and the exact location where we should place them. We went by what he said and bingo, we got all ten in one go. But then, Sir, these are rare cases. Having said that, I must also add that these rare cases keep us going.'

This kind of stuff happens only once in a while, Rajveer thought. What would he not have given to get ten terrorists in one go.

'Hmm … interesting,' he said. 'So, what do we do with this Trali? From where do we get another resource like the one you got?' he joked.

'Sir, though I have my apprehensions, I still feel we should move ahead with the information he has given us. Besides, the guy is a better bet when outside than when inside. We must follow the information given by him and see where it takes us.'

It's always good to have your team on the same wavelength as you; you work at double the speed, he thought.

Satisfied, the conversation moved to other common interests that they had, including the fitness regimes they followed. They agreed to meet every day in the gym at six-thirty in the morning to work out together. That way, they could keep each other motivated, they thought.

* * *

Over the next few days, Rajveer set in motion his plan to act on the lead Trali had given him. He and Mehak began to meet at the gym regularly and became better friends. Without his realizing it, their conversation began to border on the edge of flirtation.

Three weeks after he was invited, Maneesh boarded the Air India flight from Kabul to New Delhi and then onwards to Srinagar. Rajveer was waiting for him at the airport. They hugged each other and proceeded towards the exit meant for VIPs. Rajveer's bulletproof car and escort were at the VIP parking, waiting for them. They headed straight to Rajveer's residence.

Chapter 11

It was the month of July and it had started to rain. Maneesh was out on the balcony, sipping a refreshing cup of kahwa. While he was sipping his tea, he wondered why Rajveer had invited him to Srinagar. Over the years, they had always met in New Delhi, where Maneesh's family was based too. It was safe and had enough pubs and fine dining restaurants where they could sit and converse. Srinagar was not safe at all, especially with Rajveer, who was himself on a hit list. Whenever they met, Maneesh would ask Rajveer to relate stories from his counterterrorism activities. These stories excited him. He had always wanted to join the army or the police. He had cleared the NDA exam once but had been rejected in the medical examination because of his knock knees. At times, while listening to Rajveer's stories, Maneesh would tell him how he would have executed a task had he been in his place. He was a thorough patriot and always wanted to do something for his country.

From where he was sitting, Maneesh could see the Shankaracharya temple at a distance and wondered why this heaven on earth was witnessing so much violence. As he was finishing his kahwa, he heard the gates open and Rajveer's car entered surrounded by his posse of armed men.

Rajveer was on a call with Mehak, inviting her over for dinner at his house the following week. He hung up and headed to the balcony where Maneesh was sitting.

After some small talk, Rajveer said, 'Tell me again— how did you end up working with Afghan Airlines?'

'Well, it's a long story,' Maneesh said. 'I was travelling to the UK and was sitting in business class, and Rashid Karzai, the then president of Afghanistan, was sitting next to me. He had then been in office for barely two years and wanted to revive Afghan Airlines. Hearing that I had been a pilot for fifteen years and had also served as the general manager for ground operations, he thought I was the ideal person to take up the task of reviving the airline. When he offered me the job, I initially resisted, knowing very well the security concerns. But he told me I would have safe accommodation where all the foreign embassies are housed. He also assured me of heavy security deployment. I finally decided to accept the offer. It was not the money that mattered, but the job actually sounded exciting and challenging. And it has been. I've attended almost all the major functions at the Presidential palace, even after Karzai was replaced. I've also got the chance to meet and make friends with some of the main tribal leaders who have their own militia—even some of those in the Taliban who came to meet the President or who travelled on Afghan Airlines to exotic locations, to negotiate with the US or NATO.'

'That's interesting,' Rajveer said. He leaned forward and continued. 'Maneesh, I have some confidential work in

Afghanistan and I was thinking that you would be the best person to suggest a further course of action on this.'

Rajveer went on to explain the situation in detail. 'There is going to be a meeting at Kunduz organized by the Taliban and the ISI, and the Chinese are attending. Maulana Zaif, the deputy chief of the Lashkar-e-Jabbar, will also be there, and my source tells me the plan is to discuss how to proceed further on Kashmir. Is there any person you know in the Taliban who could help us get information on the meeting?'

Maneesh thought for a few seconds and then said with a light laugh, 'I hope I don't end up losing my life giving you this information!'

Rajveer assured him that there was nothing to worry about. 'There is no need for you to get directly involved in this. In case you think the risk is high, you can always abort the plan,' Rajveer said.

'Atif Yusufzai,' Maneesh said. 'Atif Yusufzai is the personal relations officer (PRO) to the Taliban and is present at all their meetings. He will definitely be there at this one. I know him very well.' Atif Yusufzai was a graduate of King's College London and could speak English fluently, which was rare among Talibani leaders. That was why they had chosen him as a frontman for all important functions, Maneesh knew. Rajveer too knew how important Atif Yusufzai was in the Taliban. He had met him during an international conference in Dubai a few years ago and had been impressed by the Afghani's oratorical skills.

'Will he be willing to extend help?' Rajveer asked.

'Well, money works better than anything else in Afghanistan,' Maneesh said. 'But be ready for an exorbitant demand.'

'For this, any amount of expenditure is okay,' Rajveer said.

'If that's the case,' Maneesh said, 'I'll get in touch with him as soon as I get back to Kabul.' Maneesh also knew that the Taliban was not happy with the way the Chinese were treating the Muslims of Uighur province in that country—perhaps that would work in convincing Atif to help.

'There are some basic rules you have to follow in this type of conversation,' Rajveer said. 'Our technical expert will help you out with these, and the recommended type of mobile applications that should be used. He'll come here to train you; just keep an hour free every day for that. This is essential from a safety point of view. We want this to remain hidden from the Americans as well.'

Maneesh nodded, excited and nervous about what he was being asked to do. After a while, the two friends had dinner and exchanged notes on what their old classmates were up to.

'How time flies!' Rajveer thought when he was in his bedroom later that night. Look at how many years he had now known Maneesh. Or even his time in J&K. He had expected to be posted in the Valley for two years and then reunite with his family. But it had ended up being much longer than that. Not that he was complaining. He liked to be in the thick of things and make a difference. Which Nikita had luckily understood.

It had been his and Nikita's eighteenth wedding anniversary a few days ago. And here he was, in Jammu, while Nikita was in Delhi. Life had gone through such highs and lows. He remembered his days in IIT and wondered if he had ever imagined a life like this. It was on days like this that he wished to have some stability and his family with him. He missed them very much. He also knew that this thought and these moments would pass, to be replaced with the urgency of his work. Though lonely at times like this, he was a very satisfied and content man. He was living a dream professional life. He had always wanted to be the one who called the shots and he did feel that he was contributing in a big way to the nation and the government in their fight against terror outfits.

He picked up the phone and called his wife, who gave a quick update on what was happening at home. 'The parent-teacher meeting at school went well but Niraj has been asked to work more on his mathematics. Is there any way that you can come for a few days or should we consider hiring a private tutor?'

An IITian, Rajveer abhorred the thought of having a tutor for mathematics. 'No. No tutor. Let me figure out a way to be there … though it is unlikely. Why don't you guys come over for a few days?'

'I have my clinic and patients, Rajveer. I can't just drop everything. Niraj is your child, just as much as he is mine. Plus, I anyway do a lot more for the two of them.' Nikita was clearly upset. She had been feeling overwhelmed with all the responsibilities that came with work and parenting two children in the absence of a partner.

Rajveer decided to change the topic. 'How is the planning for your school reunion coming along?' he asked, hoping to get a good response considering that she had been actively involved in the planning of the event and had been particularly excited about it.

But Nikita said, 'I'm really regretting the decision to get involved in the planning. To handle the whims and fancies of so many people and to pamper the egos of all is just not my style.'

Wrong choice, thought Rajveer. 'Hmm. What's the update on Payal?' One more attempt to change the topic.

'You are forever bothered about someone else. When was the last time you thought of me and asked about *my* well-being?'

'Nikita, what's the matter, sweetheart? What's happening?' The concern and love in Rajveer's voice was the last straw. Nikita broke down in tears. This was what he most disliked about his job—the helplessness he felt when he could not reach out and immediately hug his wife and children.

After Nikita had calmed down a little, Rajveer promised to call more often and figure out a way to visit before he hung up.

* * *

Over the next week, Maneesh visited Pahalgam, Gulmarg and Sonamarg. An avid golfer, he visited the golf course every evening, be it at Srinagar, Gulmarg or Pahalgam, and played a nine-hole. Shahid Laptop from the Crime Branch's electronic surveillance unit was assigned the task of training Maneesh on the handling of digital devices and would visit every morning for an hour to train him before he set out for office. Shahid was a communications expert and had been with the electronic surveillance unit for more than ten years. His expertise had led to many successful operations. He was constantly on his laptop and would dispatch at least two to three Quick Reaction Teams every day, based on the intelligence generated from his laptop. Hence, the name Shahid Laptop.

Maneesh was given a special mobile phone, named Infinity Pro, tailor-made for secret communications with Rajveer. Three additional phones were handed over to him for use with anyone else in Afghanistan with whom Maneesh might feel the need to hold secret communications.

'We'll get all the data from these mobile phones on our systems. So be careful to keep all your personal communication to another phone,' Rajveer said with a smile.

'At this age, data from my personal mobile will be of no use to you, be it professionally or from a gossip point of view,' Maneesh said with a laugh, and then asked, 'What if someone somehow gets hold of these phones?'

'There's a provision for remote destruction of all data on these Infinity Pro special mobile phones, which is what we'll do in case it falls into enemy hands,' Rajveer explained.

On Sunday afternoon, Maneesh boarded the Air India flight back to Delhi and then flew to Kabul. On the way from Delhi to Kabul, Maneesh wondered, again, whether he should go ahead with the plan. Thoughts of his wife and two children came to his mind. Just a week before, a member of the Human Rights Commission of Afghanistan had been killed by the Taliban, right in the heart of Kabul. The news of the killing of Zahid Habib kept going on in a loop in front of his eyes. Zahid Habib had worked for the Afghan Human Rights Commission supported by Canada, and Maneesh had met him often at functions organized by the embassy. One day, the Taliban had entered his house and killed him in front of his wife and their children. The Canadians had provided asylum to the survivors in the family and they were settled in that country now. 'We have a comfortable life, and there is no need to take a risk of this magnitude,' Maneesh said to himself. Then he thought about Rajveer and the cause he was working for. 'Maybe my actions will help save some innocent lives. If I just follow instructions, there should be very little risk,' Maneesh thought.

By the time the Air India flight landed at Kabul, Maneesh had made up his mind. He would go ahead with the plan.

***

Just as Maneesh's flight landed in Kabul, Mehak entered Rajveer's house for dinner. She was dressed in a yellow Rajasthani leheria chiffon saree and a sleeveless blouse. Her dark eyes were enhanced by the subtle use of kajal and eyeshadow. Her lips were moist with a glimmering lip colour. Rajveer could feel desire arising within him. Was it the absence of Nikita? Whatever it was, it was working. He had made sure his house was clean and had made arrangements for drinks and a simple dinner. Mehak's choice was gin and tonic, and he settled for his single malt. They talked like old friends, speaking freely about their childhood and their days in college. They were on their second drink and Rajveer couldn't remember how it had happened, but he suddenly found himself sitting next to her.

'So, tell me about your love life in college,' Mehak asked, with a flirtatious smile.

She took a sip of her drink, and a drop of it lingered on her lips. He gave her a naughty smile and, as if involuntarily, bent forward to lick the drop off her lips.

'*Tum se mil ke aisa laga tum se mil ke* ...' started to play in the background. Startled, Rajveer looked in the direction of his phone. It was the ringtone dedicated to calls from Nikita. '*Haan bolo,*' he said abruptly. He had spoken to her a couple of hours ago.

'Papa has just coughed blood,' she said, referring to his father.

The irritation changed immediately to concern and Rajveer asked, 'What? When was this?'

'He has been coughing a bit lately and I had put him on standard medication. He went to brush his teeth before going to sleep, started coughing and the next thing he knew, there was blood in the washbasin. He is really nervous. More than him, Mummy is panicking. Can you take leave for a few days and come home? I am taking him to the hospital right now,' Nikita said in a rush.

'Let me see how soon I can manage leave. Which hospital are you planning to take him to? Let me see if I can arrange for him to be seen quickly there.'

'Sanjeevani is the closest and also has a good reputation. I'm taking him there.'

'Okay. Keep me informed.'

'All right. Keep your phone with you.'

The moment between Mehak and Rajveer had passed. She asked him what had happened and he told her the situation quickly. Since he was so clearly distracted, Mehak told him she would leave without dinner. He demurred out of politeness but finally agreed. Getting help for Nikita at the hospital and ensuring that his father got the best treatment available was the topmost thing on his mind.

* * *

In Kabul, Maneesh immediately began figuring out how he could talk to Atif Yusufzai. At home, he looked at his appointments for the coming week. The Afghan National Day celebrations were coming up the following week, and all the important dignitaries based in Kabul would be invited. Atif Yusufzai was someone who was invited every year for the function.

On National Day, the Presidential palace was buzzing with activity. It was, of course, an event sans alcohol. Maneesh did a top-up with his embassy-supplied Cardhu single malt before going to attend the function. This was common among diplomats before they went to attend any Afghani function. All the ambassadors were present, with the US ambassador grabbing the most attention. The station CIA chief, the ISI representative, the Special Analysis Wing of India station head, and the British MI4 were all present, keeping an eye on each other. Though they all worked undercover, generally staying in the country under the garb of being 'counsellors', each knew everything about the other, including details of their family members and where they were located.

Maneesh reached early and kept an eye out for Atif Yusufzai. The Taliban were known for their lack of punctuality, so Maneesh was prepared for a long wait. An hour into the function, Atif finally arrived. He was a tall and imposing Afghani tribal leader in his late forties who dyed his beard black. He was wearing a traditional Afghani pagdi and the black Pathan suit typical of a Talibani.

Maneesh watched him moving around and waited. Atif first went across to the ISI officer and exchanged pleasantries. The ISI, of course, had the first claim on this man, owing to the generous amounts of money doled out, the training infrastructure and the weapons supplied to the Taliban. He then walked towards the CIA station chief, carrying his cup of herbal tea. Maneesh was close enough to hear him say to the CIA chief, 'When do we continue with the talks?' Maneesh knew Atif was referring to the peace negotiations initiated by the Americans.

'We'll let you know. It will have to be a neutral location where each one of us can talk freely,' the CIA officer replied quietly.

After half an hour, Maneesh saw Atif heading to the washroom and rushed behind him. It was the chance he'd been waiting for. No one knew which part of the hall had been bugged by the Americans, so he had wanted to avoid conversing with Atif in the main venue. Besides, mobile micro-bugging devices and cameras could be in the sherwani of the Pakistani, the suit of the M4 man, the cummerbund of the waiter, anywhere imaginable.

Maneesh occupied the urinal next to where Atif was standing and started talking.

'How is it going,' he asked.

'*Sab khairiyat hai*,' Atif replied. 'All well.' After a pause, he said, 'Can you help me upgrade my family to business class on their way to Dubai?'

'Of course, anything for you,' replied Maneesh. 'Just give me their details and travel itinerary.'

Maneesh thought he would buy business class tickets with the money provided by Rajveer, in case the upgrade was not possible.

'I needed some time with you,' Maneesh continued. 'Where and when can we meet?'

Atif looked at him curiously. Then, he finally said, 'If it's something confidential, the best place to meet is at your home. I've attended parties at your place before, so it won't look suspicious. I'll be followed to your place for sure, but no one can get inside and listen to our conversation.'

'Done. Let's meet on Tuesday evening,' Maneesh said.

Maneesh was a Hanuman bhakt, and would always choose Tuesdays to start any new project or work. 'Nothing can go wrong if Lord Hanuman is on your side,' he would say.

Tuesday morning, Maneesh took out an anti-bugging device given to him by Rajveer and scanned his house. Each corner, each painting on the wall, curtains, wallpaper, false ceiling, ceiling, sofa, doorknob—Maneesh went about checking everything as per the checklist provided to him by the experts.

Atif arrived in the evening in his luxury Toyota Fortuner, with a basket full of dry fruits for Maneesh.

Maneesh handed Atif business class tickets for his family and the two of them proceeded to chat about the current scenario in Afghanistan for some time before Maneesh finally came to the topic.

'There is a meeting planned at Kunduz, with the ISI and Chinese. Will you be there?' Maneesh asked.

Atif was taken aback and hesitated before responding. 'Why do you want to know this?' he asked.

'I thought we could make some money with the information from this meeting,' Maneesh said.

Atif was not averse to the idea. He would have looked at such an offer from any other agency with suspicion. But, coming from Maneesh, he considered it absolutely safe. Their conversations had never veered to this kind of thing in the last ten years of their acquaintance.

'Who wants the information?' Atif asked.

'I'm not allowed to reveal that right now,' Maneesh answered. If he told Atif the Indians wanted it, there was a good chance the Afghan would refuse. Maneesh was hoping Atif would think it was the US.

Atif paused and then asked, 'What kind of money are we talking about?'

'It depends on the type of information. Ask for the moon, and you might get it. Of course, I have to get my share,' Maneesh replied.

Atif laughed and agreed. He would get back on how much he wanted, he said, and would not ask for any advance. He trusted Maneesh and knew that if he made a commitment, he would honour it. Maneesh handed him an Infinity Pro phone and said any further communication between them had to take place through that instrument. 'This cannot be used for any other communication,' he said.

Atif nodded. 'The meeting is scheduled to take place next week—I'll communicate the proceedings to you,' he said.

Business done, they both headed to the dinner table, where Atif was served with gosht cooked in the Kashmiri style, while Maneesh stuck to vegetarian as he usually did on Tuesdays. Before parting, he handed Atif an expensive shahtoosh shawl, made from the wool of a rare antelope in Kashmir. Atif draped it around himself immediately and smiled. 'Looks good. Something like what Amitabh Bachchan would wear,' he said.

'Why not? You are as tall and handsome as he is,' Maneesh said. 'It looks good on you, if not better.'

Chapter 12

The test results had come in, and they were not very promising. Nikita had known from an initial scan that the situation was serious and insisted that Rajveer come to Delhi, even if it was for just a day. By the time Rajveer came, the doctors had run several tests, including a biopsy, and they told the family that it was an advanced stage of throat cancer.

With two young children and both Rajveer and Nikita working, some important decisions had to be made. The care that was required to be given to his father and the emotional support to his mother were two very different and demanding aspects of the treatment.

'We will start with eight cycles of chemotherapy. The patient needs a lot of care during and post-chemo. We must ensure that he eats healthy and his body regains strength so that he can handle the next round of chemo. You also have to be careful that he doesn't catch any infection,' the oncologist said.

Rajveer and Nikita sat in silence, listening.

On their way back home, they agreed that the children were young and exposure to what would definitely be a low atmosphere at home may not be the best for them. And perhaps their grandfather would not like to be seen in a weak condition by his grandchildren. Rajveer decided to take his parents with him to Jammu and Kashmir. His father's treatment could be undertaken there, and it would probably be easier to keep him away from infections there.

As soon as Rajveer returned to J&K, he made all the necessary arrangements for his father's treatment and his parents' stay. When he spoke to Mehak next in the office, he told her about the latest developments on the family front. It was also a subtle way of informing her that he would not be as available during his leisure time as he was earlier.

* * *

In the province of Nangrahar, in the eastern part of the country, Atif Yusufzai attended the *jirga*, tribal council meeting, of the Taliban. The leadership discussed various issues, including the ongoing peace talks with the US, and the continuing relationship with the Hekmatyar group, led by former Afghanistan prime minister Gulbuddin Hekmatyar, and the ISI.

At the jirga, Mullah Abdul Wahab, the commander of the Taliban at Kunduz, said, 'There is going to be a meeting at Kunduz between the ISI and the Chinese. Although the matter does not directly pertain to us, we have to arrange a safe house for the meeting. We also have an old ally, Maulana Zaif, coming for the meeting. He has requested us to arrange logistics for his visit and to be with him during the meeting.'

Mullah Wahab was one of the most powerful commanders in the Taliban. Even after their removal from Kabul, he had managed to retain power over the area of Kunduz, a border town near the southern boundary with Tajikistan. So much so that he was considered to be the shadow governor of Kunduz.

'Atif will be responsible for the logistics and conduct of the meeting,' Mullah Abdul Wahab said. Atif usually cribbed about being the administrative in charge, but this time he was more than happy to oblige.

Over the weekend, a convoy of Taliban along with escort vehicles entered the city of Kunduz late in the evening. The local governor received the news but chose to turn a blind eye to what was happening.

Brig. Aslam of the ISI came with his team, and Col Wang Lei from the Chinese side arrived with his men.

Maulana Zaif, who had come with Atif Yusufzai, was made to wait in the visitors' room while Brig. Aslam and Col Wang Lei discussed sensitive matters pertaining to the China–Pakistan Economic Corridor Project and the Gwadar seaport and its strategic positioning to ship Gulf oil and other key goods to and from China. They also discussed its strategic importance in enhancing the naval strength of Pakistan. Pakistan wanted to raise the issue of Muslims in Uighur province, but Col Wang Lei refused to entertain any conversation about that.

Finally, Brig. Aslam brought up the Lashkar-e-Jabbar. 'What about the proposal to support Maulana Asgar and his men in India?' he asked.

'We have a solution for them. We will help you dig tunnels across the border. The latest technology we have can be used to dig tunnels to a maximum length of 200 metres. The preconditions are that the soil should be clay and the water table should be at least 40 feet below. The technology will help you make the tunnels in two months with sufficient space in them for one man to move at a time. We will also help you with our latest drone technology, so weapons can be dropped at any given latitude and longitude, at any time.'

Brig. Aslam was ecstatic. He had a readymade solution to his problem of Lashkar-e-Jabbar men getting killed while infiltrating the border.

'And when can the process begin?' he asked.

'As soon as you fix the location as per the preconditions I just mentioned,' Col Wang Lei said. He added, 'There is one more requirement from our side, and this cannot be relayed to the Lashkar-e-Jabbar leadership. We have plans on the eastern border of India, in Kashmir. When we advance from the eastern side, you should instruct the Lashkar-e-Jabbar to use their men and material to engage from the western side so that the Indian forces are split up.'

The discussion carried on for three hours, while Maulana Zaif and Atif Yusufzai waited patiently in the visitors' room. They had finished three cups of tea by the time the talks between the ISI and the Chinese were done. Finally, the door to the conference room opened and Maulana Zaif and Atif were called inside.

Brig. Aslam introduced Atif and Maulana Zaif to Col Lei. They shook hands and Col Lei assured Maulana Zaif of their full support.

'Yes, we have a solution for all your infiltration issues now,' Brig. Aslam said. 'We'll discuss the details after our Chinese guests depart.'

Ten minutes later, the Chinese officers departed by road towards the Tajikistan border, where they had a CAIC Z-10 helicopter waiting to take them back to China.

Atif Yusufzai offered food to the remaining guests, after which they sat down at the table for discussions. Brig. Aslam had already given some thought to which areas would fulfil the soil conditions outlined by Col Lei. Only Samba and Kathua on the international border had clay soil that would enable the digging of tunnels.

'Our new route to send in your men will be from Samba,' Brig. Aslam said.

'What?' Maulana Zaif was shocked. 'But it is a Hindu-dominated area and we have no support base there,' he said.

'Had it not been a good solution, we would not have troubled you with 1000 km of travel to Kunduz,' Brig. Aslam said tersely. He explained to the maulana why they had to use Samba and then asked, 'Do you have a person in mind who will be a single point contact person for this work?'

The maulana nodded. 'Abdul Rehman Qadri. We call him ARQ. He has been our most trusted man for sending in the mujahid,' he said.

Abdul Rehman Qadri (ARQ) handled all the key tasks involved in getting men across the border. He was so trusted that even if the mujahid were killed while getting in, doubts were never raised about his integrity.

'You can send your trainees to our camps in Afghanistan till the focus on your own camps in Pakistan dies down a bit,' Atif suggested. 'We can provide our facilities at Herat and Mazar-e-Sharief for this purpose. Fifty seats in each training session will be dedicated to your men,' he said.

It was decided that ARQ would connect with Brig. Aslam regarding all future movement of Lashkar-e-Jabbar cadres across the border. Meanwhile, the ISI would coordinate with the Chinese to dig five tunnels across the border between India and Pakistan. They selected the Shakargarh sector in Pakistan, across which lay the Kathua and Samba districts of India. ARQ would also help identify suitable locations across the border where the tunnel would open.

Maulana Zaif returned to Bahawalpur under ISI escort. He headed straight to his brother and conveyed the details of the plan.

'Perfect,' Maulana Asgar said. 'We will send two batches of fresh recruits to the Taliban for training for three months. Meanwhile, let ARQ finalize locations for the tunnel with the help of our men in the Valley.'

Maulana Zaif spoke to ARQ, who began work immediately, tasking his foot soldiers and overground workers in Kashmir to move around the border and identify places that were isolated and with a reasonable forest cover where the exit of the tunnel could be planned. They were asked to send GPS coordinates of these locations when they were identified.

Meanwhile, Atif Yusufzai had headed back to Kabul. Once there, and alone at home, he took out the Infinity Pro and typed a message: 'Meeting successful. Let's meet and discuss.'

The special electronic surveillance unit control room in Srinagar beeped and a red light flashed. The operator rushed to Rajveer's office, and said, 'Sir, there is a message on the Infinity Pro.'

Rajveer immediately headed to the control room and looked at the message.

'Is this the unit with Maneesh?' he asked.

'No, sir. This is a different one,' the operator said.

'This means Maneesh is on the job and the plan is moving forward,' Rajveer told himself. He typed out a message to Maneesh on the Infinity Pro. 'Avoid meeting very often in person. The Infinity Pro is safe and you can speak to your man on this set.'

From his experience in counterterrorist operations, Rajveer knew that any unusual movement or meetings between two people beyond the normal would invite attention. Kabul had not one but many intelligence agencies working on the same set of people.

Maneesh read the message and smiled. 'They have the information in Srinagar,' he thought.

'By the way, who is this person?' Rajveer texted.

'Atif Yusufzai, the spokesperson of the Taliban,' Maneesh replied.

'Great!' Rajveer said. 'This is the jackpot if you are able to sustain things.'

Taking Rajveer's advice, Maneesh texted Atif, 'Call me on the Infinity Pro when you are alone.'

Atif called back late that night.

'*As salaam alaikum*, Maneesh bhai,' he said.

'*Walekum as salaam*,' Maneesh replied.

'There is a lot to share,' Atif said. 'Interesting developments at the meeting.'

Atif had been surprised himself at the conversation that had taken place. He knew the Chinese would help the Lashkar-e-Jabbar in some way, but the digging of tunnels was unexpected. He explained in detail all that had been decided in Kunduz: the plan to dig tunnels with the help of the Chinese; to send in mujahideen from Samba; and the roles of Brig. Aslam, Abdul Rehman Qadri and the key Lashkar-e-Jabbar commander.

'That's excellent,' said Maneesh. 'We need to find ways to keep the information channel open. How do we do this?'

'I assumed this would be your next question,' Atif said. 'And I have made arrangements for that too.'

Atif explained his offer to train Lashkar-e-Jabbar cadres, which had been readily accepted by Maulana Zaif. 'We can try to tap a boy among the trainees. He will be our asset in the Lashkar-e-Jabbar.'

Rajveer was listening to all this in real time in Srinagar. 'Is there any timeline?' he texted Maneesh.

Maneesh repeated the question to Atif.

'It does not look like anything will happen soon. They have to identify a suitable place, dig the tunnels ... all that should take at least six months,' Atif said. 'By that time, the first batch of the Lashkar-e-Jabbar will also be trained at Herat and Mazar-e-Sharief.'

'Can we keep track of the activities of Abdul Rehman Qadri?' Rajveer texted Maneesh, who repeated it to Atif.

'That won't be possible. Although our relationship with Maulana Zaif is good, we cannot take the risk of keeping a watch on Qadri. Let us not get too adventurous,' Atif said.

'Ask him about the payment. Is he okay with cash through hawala?' typed Rajveer.

'Afghanistan runs on cash,' Atif said when Maneesh posed the question. 'No one exchanges currency in the banks here. It's at the Kabul money market on the banks of the Kabul River near the blue mosque where all the money exchanges hands. Send the money there to the shop of the Sikh gentleman, Sunny Singh.'

Although any deal through hawala entailed a commission of 2 per cent for the dealer, no one charged the Taliban any commission.

Having spent more than ten years in Kabul, Maneesh knew the place well. Stockpiles of cash on the footpath, cash in gunny bags and currency of all denominations and countries were common at that place. The law of the land did not prevail in Afghanistan. It was only tribal practices that were followed.

'Sending $100,000 right away to Sunny Singh,' typed Rajveer. 'It will reach in half an hour.'

Maneesh conveyed this to Atif.

'That was quick,' Atif said.

'This is just the beginning,' Maneesh said.

'*Inshallah*,' Atif replied.

Chapter 13

Rajveer was busy on the home front as well. His father's treatment had begun and was fortunately going well. His mother had also become more accepting of the situation and had taken over the running of the house.

Mehak was getting transferred to another posting, and life felt a little monotonous for Rajveer. The only highlight of his life was his sessions at the gym and the food on his table, cooked by his mother. At the other end of his world, Nikita was finding herself more irritated these days than otherwise. Her work at the clinic had increased, and she had two children to take care of. She needed a vacation, which she couldn't take. She found herself getting into more arguments with Rajveer than usual.

'Let's wait a month. Papa's break before the next chemo session will come in three weeks. You use this time to organize your patients. At the end of this month, let's take a short break. Too much has been happening and we need to spend some time together,' Rajveer suggested, and it came like a fresh breeze to Nikita; she felt happy to have something to look forward to.

* * *

A month later, the first batch of trainees arrived in pickup vans at the Taliban training centre at Herat.

Atif Yusufzai was a regular at the training camps, teaching the trainees how to figure out what a person was thinking from their body language. 'Jihad is not a simple, straightforward task,' he would say. 'For a jihadi to survive an adverse situation, you have to understand the psyche of every person you come in contact with, and what they are thinking. There have been instances when a trusted person is discovered as working for the adversary, which leads to heavy losses.'

As Atif took the classes, he was constantly on the lookout for potential candidates for Maneesh. Being a good judge of people and an expert at reading body language, he shortlisted a couple of them. As part of the regular training, he called each of the trainees during the lunch break to his room. He interviewed them one by one, asking about their background, family history, qualifications, financial status and motivation for jihad.

One of them, Salman Rashid, was from an affluent family and said he wanted to join jihad for the sake of Islam and his duty to act against kafirs. Another had five brothers and was motivated by revenge for what he called the *shahadat* (martyrdom) of his elder brother at the hands of security forces in Kashmir. Among the trainees was Khalid Jutt, a strong Punjabi boy barely twenty-two years old. Atif found out that Khalid was from a very poor family. He was the only boy—he had three sisters—and had been told by his recruiters that the family would be supported financially for his contribution to jihad. They had also said that he could return home after completing two years in the Kashmir Valley.

Khalid Jutt stood out among all the interviewees, Atif thought, and he called him to his residence one evening.

'It's good to know that you are dedicated to a great cause,' Atif started.

Khalid shrugged and remained silent.

Atif smiled and said, 'So, why have you joined, if not for the cause?'

'For the financial stability of my family,' Khalid replied. 'I just want to finish my two years and then I'll return to them.'

'Do you know the average lifespan of a mujahid?' Atif asked.

Khalid shook his head.

'A year and a half,' Atif said.

'But … they told me I could go back after two years,' Khalid said.

'Son, life on this path is difficult, but we are all here to fight for a cause,' Atif said. 'If you are lucky, you may come back alive.'

'I have to go back after completing my task—I have to take care of my sisters and mother,' Khalid said, upset.

'Then let me think of some work for you at the Lashkar-e-Jabbar office at Bahawalpur,' Atif said. 'That way, you can dedicate yourself to the cause and be safe at the same time.'

'I am not a well-read man, but I can do any physical work given to me,' Khalid said.

Atif sent out a message to Maulana Zaif, requesting an office job for Khalid Jutt on compassionate grounds. Maulana Zaif agreed, saying he could clean and act as a general peon at the Lashkar-e-Jabbar office in Bahawalpur.

Atif conveyed the news to Khalid, who was thrilled.

Khalid continued to train for the next three months. He met Atif Yusufzai on all three occasions when he visited to deliver lectures to the trainees. By the end of the training, Khalid was completely under Atif's spell; he saw him as his godfather. After the valedictory session, Atif called Khalid for dinner and spoke to him at length.

'Keep me informed about any important issues at Bahawalpur. You understand—we each need to know about the other's functioning to coordinate better,' Atif said, careful not to say anything that could be interpreted as an attempt at spying. 'We will support you with an additional twenty thousand rupees every month for your efforts.'

Atif went on to say that the Lashkar-e-Jabbar commanders were very suspicious by nature and that any communication with him had to be on an Internet call. Atif gifted him an Android phone with the Echochat app downloaded.

As per standard practice, all the trainees were sent home for a week as a rest period. This was also the time given to them to tie up loose ends before they moved forward on the unknown and uncertain journey of jihad.

Khalid went to his home town at Gujranwala for his rest period and then left for Bahawalpur. He handed his family one lakh rupees, given to him by Atif Yusufzai, so their expenses could be met while he was away.

On reaching Bahawalpur, he was briefed on his duties by the officer-in-charge. He was given a room at the rear end of the office, where the security guards also lived. They had a common kitchen for all the staff and an executive kitchen for the core team of the Lashkar-e-Jabbar. 'So, there is a class system among the jihadis too,' Khalid thought to himself.

* * *

In Kabul, Atif was in touch with Maneesh, briefing him about the progress in recruiting Khalid. Whether it worked well or not depended on how Khalid behaved after joining the office at Bahawalpur, Atif said. If Khalid was sharp and was able to perform, the plan would work. 'The Lashkar-e-Jabbar does not include the helpers for the Friday preaching. Good thing for us. Had they done that, they could have easily turned Khalid into a loyalist. Such is the power they have in the way they preach. Since he will not be a part of it, I am hoping that he will start delivering sooner rather than later.'

Maneesh had been trained well. Rajveer had told him: his job was to listen and let Atif speak. So he did just that. He would ask questions now and then, and prompt only when more information was needed. He waited for a while, giving Atif the space to add something if he wanted to, and then said, 'Let's hope for the best,' before hanging up.

At the other end, Rajveer was listening and was very happy with the progress. He called Maneesh and said, 'This is good work. The guy Atif seems useful and effective. We have the system in place, and I think this should work. We have done our part; now let's leave the rest to God.' Rajveer closed his eyes as he said this, and then added, 'Another sum of hundred thousand dollars will reach Atif in the next month.' He hung up, and then texted almost immediately, 'I will also send some to you in cash.'

Chapter 14

Over the years, the border trade facility at Chakoti had continued to thrive.

Chaudhary Alam, the trade facilitator for the politician Hamad Lone at the border, was busy counting the number of banana and spice trucks that went across to Pakistan and the number of almond trucks that were coming in. While doing so, he constantly watched out for a truck that had a Pathan shoe hanging from the front bonnet. When the truck arrived, he indicated to the security officer at the checkpost to have a closer look at it.

The truck was taken to one side and the driver was frisked.

'Please take care of the traffic congestion while we search the truck,' the security officer, Maqbool, requested Chaudhary Alam.

'*Chalo, chalo, chalo,*' Alam indicated to the trucks behind the target truck. In a hurry, twenty trucks followed and crossed the border, the security guards just giving them a cursory glance.

'What's there in the truck?' Maqbool asked the truck driver.

'Nothing but almonds,' the driver replied. 'It's meant for Sajjad Traders.'

Maqbool asked his men to check the truck thoroughly, confident that the information from Chaudhary Alam could never be wrong.

And sure enough, the security personnel found a cavity on the inside of a mudguard. A mechanic was called to strip it open.

Inside, they found 500 gm of heroin and two pistols carefully camouflaged. It was a good catch. The heroin was worth Rs 50 lakh in the international market. The pistols indicated a narco terror module operating from across the border. The driver was taken to the nearby Special Operations Group camp and questioned, but even after three days, the SOG was unable to get anything out of him.

'He really does not appear to have any knowledge about the consignment. But how is that possible?' Maqbool asked Chaudhary Alam.

'I don't know. The information was provided by a source who is across the border and was associated with the Lashkar-e-Jabbar earlier,' Alam replied.

Investigations into the narco terror case hit a dead end and the driver got bail after a few days of detention. The truck got released by Sajjad Traders, through their advocate.

The evening of the big catch at the Chakoti border, Hamad Lone threw a party at his palatial bungalow at Uri for the police officials. As a sitting PDF minister, he was well known to the army personnel and the local brigade commander, Sandeep Khosla, also attended the party.

The most expensive single malts were being served. While the brigade commander enjoyed his single malt, Hamad Lone stuck to a vodka mixed with Limca to camouflage the alcohol. Chaudhary Alam requested a Merlot, which was promptly served from Hamad Lone's bar. The minister's enviable collection of alcohol had been accumulated over numerous trips abroad 'for rest'. Maqbool was in a corner, drinking Old Monk mixed with Coke. The gathering was too high profile for him. His boss, Imtiaz, the local SSP, a stylish man wearing a cowboy hat, sipped his choice of single malt with the brigade commander. There were very few Muslim officers in the Kashmir Valley who would sip their alcohol unabashedly and with confidence.

The party continued till late in the night. Dinner was laid out at midnight, when everyone had been drinking for hours. Everyone minus two! Chaudhary Alam and Hamad Lone kept their drinks to a minimum so they could discuss business after the guests had left. At the dinner table, Brig. Sandeep Khosla repeated the famous quote from the movie *Shaurya*: '*Fauji ki life mein sirf do cheezen hoti hain. Shaurya aur single malt.*' [There are only two things in the life of a soldier. Valour and single malt.]

Hamad Lone raised a toast to the statement.

'Cheers to an excellent police operation!' Chaudhary Alam said.

Everyone present clicked glasses while Imtiaz smiled, acknowledging the praise for the action in which he had no role to play.

After dinner was over, the guests slowly dispersed. Hamad Lone bowed ten degrees extra at the time of bidding goodbye, excited at the thought of finding out from Chaudhary Alam what the haul had been. He knew there was something good in the offing.

When only the two of them were left, Hamad Lone asked his gunmen to leave and took Chaudhary Alam into the drawing room. With an expression befitting someone who knew they had achieved good results, Chaudhary Alam took out a chit from his pocket and read out: 'Fifteen kg of heroin, seven AK-47 rifles, seven pistols, thirty grenades, magazines and ammunition.' He continued, 'The heroin would be worth at least fifteen crore in the market.'

'Do we have a buyer for the heroin?'

'Yes. I have finalized it with couriers at Jammu, who will hand them over to the Nigerians at Pathankot,' Alam said. 'The courier will charge two lakh rupees per kilogram for the service.'

'Where have you kept the weapons?' Lone asked.

'It has been received by Zafarullah's men at Srinagar from Sajjad Traders,' Alam said, adding, 'Each of the seven trucks that passed after the truck that was searched had one AK-47, one pistol, two packets of heroin and ammunition.'

The net result of the entire operation was that it was a win-win situation for all involved: the police got a decent catch of drugs and arms, the Lashkar-e-Jabbar got its share of arms and ammunition, and Hamad Lone and Chaudhary Alam had their huge share of money from the smuggled drugs. The Pakistanis charged Rs 15 lakh per kilogram for the heroin smuggled in, which was paid through Hamad Lone's business establishments in Dubai. The money earned through the trade was extra and quietly adjusted by Zafarullah in the NGO he'd set up, Al Shafa Trust, showing it as donations by Dubai- and India-based

firms largely owned by Hamad Lone and shell companies
of the Lashkar-e-Jabbar in Saudi Arabia and Malaysia.

Weapons continued to come in through this trade
route established by Hamad Lone. The strategy used by
Chaudhary Alam—of letting one small consignment be
intercepted while pushing in the larger packages of arms
and drugs—was very successful. The local police were
happy, as they were praised for their efforts in seizing the
contraband.

A part of the smuggled heroin was distributed through
small drug peddlers in the Kashmir Valley, which fetched
them a sale rate of at least Rs 2 crore per kilogram. Hamad
Lone and Chaudhary Alam now had immense amounts
of money.

Hamad Lone had once read the book *Killing Pablo*. He
had realized that it was possible to make billions out of
the drug trade, but that it was a highly risky method with
terrible consequences if one were caught. He thought he
could balance it out by making less out of the trade and
keeping a low profile, unlike Pablo Escobar. And the route
he took was opposite to what Escobar had taken. Hamad
Lone first became a minister and then entered the drug
trade, whereas Escobar first became a drug lord and then
tried to use that money and muscle power to become a
minister and gain legitimacy. Therefore, Hamad Lone was
definitely better placed and safer, he felt.

The Lashkar-e-Jabbar cadres soon had a ready
stockpile of weapons available in the Valley. They could
travel light with minimum weaponry and reach the Valley
where Manzoor Trali and Zafarullah had a well-established
structure of overground workers.

By now, two tunnels were complete and digging was going on at two more places. The Lashkar-e-Jabbar decided to push in their men. A meeting was called at the Bahawalpur office, which Rashid Latif and Kashif Mohammed attended, along with Maulana Zaif, ARQ and Maulana Majid Asgar. It had been a very long time since the participants from Shakargarh had been able to have a meeting in person.

'It's time to send in our trained men to support our brothers in the Kashmir Valley,' Khalid Jutt heard Maulana Asgar say, while serving them tea.

'We'll need small oxygen cylinders for the men who will move through the tunnels, as well as helmets with headlights,' ARQ said.

'Leave that to the ISI,' said Maulana Asgar. 'We will have to communicate to them the dates of travel, so we move without hindrance at the border.'

'We'll also have to select the first two batches of trained mujahideen in the next few days, while it is a dark night cycle as per the lunar calendar,' interjected Maulana Zaif.

'This is what they are forever planning,' Khalid thought. He did not consider the conversation of enough significance to report it to his mentor, Atif Yusufzai.

Two months passed and five groups of mujahideen sneaked in through the tunnels. They were received by Lashkar-e-Jabbar cadres on the Indian side and ferried to the Valley. There, they were taken care of by none other than Manzoor Trali, who arranged everything, including reception, boarding, lodging and planning.

Over the months, Manzoor had carried on in as normal a way as possible, like any other citizen going about his daily chores. He even utilized the status of a pir given to him by others, visiting houses of officers when they were unwell or when they needed some local '*totka*', divine intervention, for their problems. He kept up his business of loading cement from Jammu and transporting it to the Kashmir Valley, but this was just a cover to move infiltrating terrorists. All the communication with the Lashkar-e-Jabbar was done through encrypted applications on the mobile. He had remained in touch with Rajveer, as well as high-ranking officials of the BSF and other security forces, and no one suspected that he was actually still involved in terrorist activities.

Now, Manzoor conducted a reconnaissance of security force camps and the security around political people whom the Lashkar-e-Jabbar believed worked against their interests. In February 2018, the Lashkar-e-Jabbar carried out a deadly IED explosion on a Central Armed Police Force (CAPF) convoy at Budgam, which killed thirty personnel. Hearing the news on a satellite phone, Maulana Asgar was elated. 'It's time now for another decisive blow,' he said to his brother.

'Yes. The martyrdom of our brethren cannot go to waste,' replied Maulana Zaif.

The Lashkar-e-Jabbar had suffered setback after setback, and now they wanted vengeance.

At Srinagar, a high-level meeting was held at the Chashma Shahi conference room, which was headed by the interior minister. Clearly upset with the huge loss of lives, he asked all present to go all out in the war against terrorism. The DGP held a follow-up meeting after the minister had left, and asked everyone to activate all sources

to target the Lashkar-e-Jabbar. Towards the end of the
meeting, he took Rajveer—his most trusted and reliable
man—to one side and told him that this was a matter of
prestige and that he needed to do something.

Rajveer went back to his office and called up Maneesh
on the Infinity Pro.

'Is there anything we have on the Lashkar-e-Jabbar
and their attack on the convoy at Budgam?' he asked.

Maneesh replied in the negative. There had been no
information from Atif and his contact at Bahawalpur.
Rajveer asked Maneesh to talk to Atif, and after hanging
up, he tasked his officers to keep a watch on all listed
overground workers of the Lashkar-e-Jabbar and report
about their activities.

Maneesh messaged Atif on the Infinity Pro, asking him
to call him back when free. Atif called back immediately.
Maneesh asked him if there had been any information
from his contact about the Budgam attack.

Atif knew by now who Maneesh was working for, but
by the time he had figured it out, the instalments of cash
payments were too generous to give up. In any case, he told
himself, the Taliban had no great bond with the Lashkar-
e-Jabbar. He replied now that he would contact his man
and get back.

When he spoke to Khalid Jutt, Atif instructed him to
convey the general activities of the Lashkar-e-Jabbar and
also to report back on any conversation about infiltration,
whether he thought it was of significance or not.

At the Bahawalpur headquarters, ARQ, Rashid and
Kashif celebrated the success of the attack. People turned
up in large numbers to congratulate them. Khalid went

around, serving the guests. At night, he connected with Atif Yusufzai and told him about the celebrations and the attendees. He also sent a picture of Maulana Zaif blessing some of the invitees. Atif could now connect the dots and was sure that the Budgam attack was carried out by the Lashkar-e-Jabbar. He thanked Khalid and asked him to try to get more information regarding the Lashkar-e-Jabbar's plans. He told Khalid that he was sending Rs 50,000 for his family. It would be delivered to his house in two days.

The information given by Khalid was quickly passed on to Maneesh. He reported it to Rajveer, who was happy that information had started trickling in from Lashkar-e-Jabbar headquarters.

A few days later, Khalid overheard what he knew would be useful information for Atif.

'Let's send the best three of our team for the attack in Jammu. This time it should be at Patnitop,' he heard Maulana Asgar say. The maulana knew that any attack at Patnitop—a popular tourist destination—was bound to lead to communal clashes, which would bleed Jammu and Kashmir further.

'Abu Bakar, Qari Yunus and Abu Qital would be ideal for this,' said Maulana Zaif.

The trio had returned from the training camp at Herat and had been adjudged the best in the advanced course. Khalid had been among the ones who did the worst. The Lashkar-e-Jabbar had criteria very different from other organizations while ranking their trainees. The first and most important criterion was the understanding of the holy text as explained to them by the Taliban trainers. Then came the indoor test results, which included an understanding of the latest in communication, team-building, handling of GPS and satellite phones, and finally, physical fitness and handling of weapons.

The chosen three—Abu Bakar, Qari Yunus and Abu Qital—were fond of riding motorbikes and were always seen on their favourite Sigma YCR 150s. Maulana Zaif had therefore named them the BYQ (pronounced 'bike') gang, putting the first letter of their surnames together. It was decided that the BYQ gang would carry out the major assault, and they were called for a briefing at Bahawalpur HQ.

Chapter 15

The BYQ gang reached Bahawalpur early in the morning and offered namaz together in the local mosque. They then headed to the Lashkar-e-Jabbar headquarters, where they were met by Maulana Zaif.

'The plan is to let you in from the Samba sector across the Shakargarh border. Ashiq Ahmed of Pulwama will receive you after you have entered through the tunnel. ARQ will be in charge of launching you from our side. We will explain the exact plans to you a day before you head in,' the maulana said. The Lashkar-e-Jabbar's philosophy was simple: they kept the plan close to their chest and only disclosed details to the executors just before they had to be implemented.

Khalid walked in with a tray of Kashmiri roti and chai. The elite and the mediocre were meeting for the first time since the training. The BYQ gang began to make fun of him. Mockingly they shared memories of his repeated failed attempts to clear the course in religious studies.

Maulana Zaif laughed along with them and said with pride that the Lashkar-e-Jabbar did not accept anyone who was found wanting on this front.

Khalid felt humiliated but remained silent. 'Come and have a wrestling session and see what I can do to you,' he thought to himself.

Ignited by their behaviour, when he was alone, Khalid called Atif Yusufzai in Kabul on Echochat. 'Maulana Zaif is sending the BYQ gang to Kashmir,' he said.

Atif knew the BYQ gang from the training days at Herat.

'They have a special plan for the Jammu side,' he continued.

'Any other information on this?' Atif asked.

'The only thing I heard is that they will get in from the Shakargarh side and some Ashiq Ahmed of Pulwama will receive them,' he replied. 'I can try and find out the exact date when they will get in.'

Atif passed on this information to Maneesh. Rajveer's team was excited—finally, they were getting a solid lead from Khalid.

Rajveer called an emergency meeting of his core team and tasked them with finding Ashiq Ahmed of Pulwama who had links with the Lashkar-e-Jabbar. He then called Maneesh and told him to keep in frequent touch with Atif to get the exact dates of the infiltration. He knew that, even if the information was not specific, he would be able to track the terrorists if the exact date of infiltration was known, and if there was only one overground worker from Pulwama by the name of Ashiq Ahmed.

The core team started working on all possible overground workers, surrendered terrorists and their family members, those who had served their sentences and been released from jail. The terror groups invariably looked for this connection to develop contacts and an overground structure to carry out their activities. After a day's hectic efforts, they listed twenty individuals with the names Ashiq Ahmed, Ashfaq Ahmed and Ashaq Ahmed from the database available to them. They left no stone unturned while scrutinizing call records, travel data and mobile numbers in the numerous call records of Lashkar-e-Jabbar terrorists available in their database.

While they were searching for Ashiq, the thought of Manzoor Trali came to Rajveer's mind. After all, Manzoor Trali had been a very important member of the Lashkar-e-Jabbar. 'Maybe it is Manzoor Trali who arranged that Ashiq should work for the Lashkar-e-Jabbar. Or perhaps it is Trali himself being referred to as Ashiq by the Lashkar-e-Jabbar,' thought Rajveer.

He asked for Trali's call records and scrutinized his movement pattern. Trali had visited Jammu on twenty-five occasions in the past and was generally in and around south Kashmir for the rest of the time. Rajveer went through the movement pattern in and around the date of the attack at Budgam. Usually, one looks for a person's presence around the attack site or an abrupt switching off of the mobile phone. Trali's mobile was on and he had been in Tral during the period. Right now, he was in Ajmer, Rajveer saw. He asked his team to call Trali over to the office once he returned from Ajmer.

There was one mobile number belonging to Ashiq Ahmed that appeared in three different call records of known terrorists. His movement pattern was analysed, and it was found that he had visited Jammu thrice in the past month. From the information they had on him, they saw that he owned a truck in which he shipped cement from a warehouse in Samba to Kashmir. What stood out from his last visit was that he had taken a detour from the national highway and headed towards the border an hour past midnight. This was highly unusual for someone purporting to be transporting cement.

Rajveer's covert team, Charlie 1, was assigned a twenty-four-hour surveillance on the individual. The team had sub-teams. They stuck to the common practice of pairing a male and a female member in the sub-teams. The sub-team comprised young members who posed as newlywed couples. To make it look authentic, they would demonstrate affection, hugging and touching each other as any normal newlywed couple on their honeymoon would do.

* * *

In Kabul, Maneesh called Atif over to his house for dinner and discussed the developments. Maneesh assured Atif that another hundred thousand dollars would reach Sunny Singh at the Kabul money market in the next twenty-four hours. 'But the date of infiltration is essential,' he added.

'*Inshallah*, we will know the exact date,' Atif replied.

A week later, Maneesh received a call on his Infinity Pro from Atif.

'They will get in on the third day of the new moon, as per the lunar calendar,' Atif said.

Rajveer's team calculated the date—it worked out to 8 August.

Surveillance on the national highway increased. The border guarding forces were alerted, as was the team trailing Ashiq Ahmed.

On 6 August, at 10 a.m., a truck driven by a man called Muneer started from Arihal, Pulwama and headed towards Galandar Chowk. It then turned right, towards Anantnag. Midway to Anantnag, it stopped at Bijbehara, where Ashiq Ahmed boarded the truck as a helper.

Team Charlie 1 got into action immediately. It followed the truck closely in a Maruti van. Shabnam and Vishal of the first sub-team of Charlie 1 also followed the truck in a Hyundai i10. Shabnam was dressed in a red salwar kameez, and red bangles adorned both her wrists. The second sub-team, well-equipped with assault rifles, followed 2 km behind in an Alto. They all knew very well that, for any special assignment, the Lashkar-e-Jabbar had a group of spotters to track if they were being followed.

The truck turned right from Achabal Chowk and headed towards Jawahar Tunnel. Then, after passing through the tunnel, it stopped. Ashiq Ahmed got down and looked around. He waited for some vehicles to pass and then boarded the truck again. Shabnam and Vishal were in one of the vehicles that passed the truck; they moved ahead, glancing at the truck in the rear-view mirror.

By the time the truck reached Udhampur, it was dark and it was easier for the Charlie 1 teams to take turns to follow the vehicle.

The truck finally stopped at a cement warehouse at Bari Brahmna. Ashiq took out some documents and handed them over to the warehouse in-charge. They exchanged a few words, after which Ashiq and the truck driver checked into a nearby hotel.

The Charlie 1 teams took turns keeping an eye on the hotel while ensuring that they were not noticed. The next morning, 7 August, Ashiq returned to the warehouse and filled the truck with cement bags. While doing so, he carefully created space between the bags sufficient to house four men. He kept blankets, a towel and a set of clothes in the cavity for each mujahid. The cavity also had access to the small door on the side of the truck.

Across the border, the BYQ gang assembled at Shakargarh. ARQ had briefed them about the movement, the route to be taken, the receiver on the Indian side and their subsequent movement ahead to Patnitop. Weapons, grenades, IEDs, a GPS device, an ammunition pouch, dry rations and shoes had been provided to each member, sufficient for a fidayeen to sustain at least a two-day battle. They had studied the tourist destination Patnitop on Google Maps and were told to try to take hostages after the first round of firing. The Lashkar-e-Jabbar had important commanders in jail whom they wanted to be released.

At midnight, all three fidayeen assembled at the border across the Samba sector. They messaged Ashiq Ahmed on the Dialog app: 'Reaching by 4 a.m.'

Before entering the tunnel, they undertook the customary rituals of a fidayeen attacker. They shaved themselves completely clean, ate their meals and then entered the tunnel with their backpacks, a few empty sandbags and one oxygen cylinder each. They were accompanied by one associate, who carried the extra luggage for them.

The men exited the tunnel in half an hour and saw dense bushes around them. Some distance ahead was the BSF sentry post, with the sentry looking towards the well-lit fence protecting the border from infiltrators.

When all three attackers were out, the associate retreated with the oxygen cylinders. The attackers closed the mouth of the tunnel with the sandbags they had brought with them and then covered it with twigs and leaves. Abu Qital then took out a GPS device on which was mapped the route that would take them to the roadhead at the national highway where Ashiq Ahmed was waiting.

* * *

Ashiq Ahmed had been constantly checking his message app. He was nervous. In all previous transfers of mujahids after infiltration, he had taken them straight to the Kashmir Valley. They were dropped in an area in south Kashmir that was considered their stronghold. This was the first time that he had to take the attackers straight to the site where they would carry out a suicide attack. He feared getting apprehended or killed.

At midnight, a message flashed that the guests had set off from their base. He immediately began to get things ready. He woke up Muneer and together they put packed food inside the cavity in the truck. Then, they set off towards the pre-decided location on the national highway.

* * *

It had been a busy night for Rajveer and his team. Every movement, every second, every moment was critical and was being dealt with as such.

His technical team was continuously monitoring the Internet activity on Ashiq Ahmed's mobile phone. Though they had not been able to get the content, they were sure that Ashiq Ahmed was awake at midnight and active on the Internet. The Charlie 1 teams were alerted.

At around 2.45 a.m., the truck with Muneer and Ashiq emerged out of the warehouse, took a left turn and headed towards Samba. They reached Basantar rivulet at 3.30 a.m., took a U-turn and stopped near a signboard that read 'SRINAGAR 310 kms'.

The Charlie 1 teams had been following with a new set of vehicles and commandos. Shabnam and Vishal had been now replaced by Anju and Shafi, and they all kept watch from a distance. At around 3.40 a.m., the BYQ gang emerged from the nearby bushes. Ashiq got down from his truck, briefly exchanged words with them and took a packet that one of the men handed to him. The packet contained two IEDs for another module of the Lashkar-e-Jabbar to pick up. Ashiq had been told to drop it at a particular place, by the roadside. Dropping a weapons consignment or an IED consignment in a predetermined location was standard modus operandi for the Lashkar-e-Jabbar. The idea behind this was to keep the two modules, the dropper and the picker, secret from each other. Ashiq was not aware of it, but the plan was to use the IED later on, in twin blasts in Jammu city.

Having taken the packet, Ashiq opened the side door of the truck. The attackers climbed inside, after which he shut the door and clamped it.

The truck pulled on to the road and headed towards the Kashmir Valley. The Charlie 1 team immediately alerted the Quick Reaction Team (QRT) that had been strategically placed at the Ban toll plaza to take on the terrorists if required. That team had bulletproof vehicles, surveillance drones and the best of weapons, including multiple grenade launchers. All vehicles had to stop at the toll plaza compulsorily to pay the toll, and the place was well-lit, giving an advantage to the counterterror teams.

Rajveer's tech team had been keeping track of Dialog app activity at three locations. One by the Lashkar-e-Jabbar commander across the border, one by Ashiq Ahmed, who was talking to the commander, and a third one in the Kashmir Valley. Any Dialog app activity at this time of the night in the Kashmir Valley was extremely suspicious.

Ashiq Ahmed stopped the truck near Sidhra and dropped the packet the BYQ gang had given him near a transmission tower on the roadside. He then quickly took a selfie against the road signage and posted it for the Lashkar-e-Jabbar commanders. He swiftly switched off the mobile and moved on. The other two Dialog communications continued.

Rajveer was alert, keeping an eye on the activities of each member of his team from his control room. While the tech team was on the same premises and continuously updated him on the goings-on, he watched the big screen on his office wall, which showed the movement of the two Charlie teams. He got a little worried when the two teams stopped near Sidhra.

'What's happening?' he asked Shafi from the Charlie 1 sub-team.

'Sir, the truck has stopped and Ashiq has come out,' he said, adding, 'He has dropped a packet in the bushes by the roadside.'

Shafi had noticed the packet in Ashiq's hand.

When the truck started moving again, Shafi informed Rajveer. He dropped two people to keep a watch in the area to identify and pick up anyone who came to get that packet.

The truck reached Ban toll plaza at 4.45 a.m. and was signalled to stop by the side by the QRT. The rear team of the QRT provided cover to the interception team behind a bulletproof bunker with the muzzle of a light machine gun pointing towards the truck.

Ashiq kept his cool and got down from the truck.

'What's inside the vehicle?' Inspector Tahir Saleem, who was heading the QRT team, asked in a gruff and commanding tone.

'Cement bags,' replied Ashiq, matter-of-factly.

'Can I have a look at the papers?' asked Tahir, in an equally matter-of-fact way.

Ashiq signalled to Muneer to come down with the papers.

Tahir glanced at the papers and then asked Ashiq to open the side door of the truck. Ashiq hesitated but moved to open the door. Abu Bakar, Yunus and Qital had been alert the moment the truck came to a halt. They peeped from a gap between the wooden planks and saw Ashiq walk towards the door along with another man.

Abu Bakar switched on his mobile and messaged the Lashkar-e-Jabbar commanders on Dialog: 'Trouble', he wrote. The three then cocked their weapons and waited, holding their breath,

Before Ashiq could open the door, all three fired at Tahir who was standing next to Ashiq. A bullet hit Tahir's bulletproof jacket and ricocheted. Another one found the gap on the side of the jacket and hit Tahir in the abdomen. A bulletproof Scorpio quickly moved in to provide cover and pick up Tahir. In the melee, Ashiq jumped towards the ravines on the side and escaped.

The firefight continued for some time, but finally, the BYQ gang had nowhere to go. All three mujahideen were killed in a short gun battle. Muneer was apprehended and he could disclose nothing, except the name of the co-passenger. In fact, true to the tactics of the terrorists, each overground worker knew very little about the activity of the others.

ARQ, waiting on the other side of the border at Shakargarh, sent out a message to Manzoor Trali: 'Pray to Allah for the mujahideen. They are in trouble. The reception team should retreat.'

'Tell everyone to switch off their mobiles and remain underground for some time,' Trali wrote and switched off his mobile.

'Sir, there are six Dialog users in the Kashmir Valley at this time, out of which only two are in south Kashmir,' the tech team told Rajveer. 'It should not be very difficult to identify them. One of the two in south Kashmir must be in the reception team for the terrorists.'

Rajveer asked his team to send in first aid for Tahir and to fly in an MI 17 helicopter to evacuate him. Within an hour, the helicopter was at the Ban toll plaza and Tahir was airlifted to the Army base hospital, where he was immediately taken to the operation theatre for surgery.

Rajveer messaged Maneesh in Kabul: 'Mission accomplished'. He then assigned a team to start the investigation and tie up the loose ends. The packet dropped at Sidhra by Ashiq was recovered by the team and two heavy 5 kg IEDs were seized. The Lashkar-e-Jabbar aborted the plan for the IED blasts in Jammu and asked the person going to pick it up to stay away once they received the alert message from Abu Bakar. Rajveer then immediately headed towards the base hospital to check on Tahir.

After surgery, Tahir was taken to the recovery room.

'We're fortunate,' said the doctor. 'The bullet pierced his abdomen, but did not damage any vital part.'

Rajveer waited for Tahir to regain consciousness and then, putting his hand on his head, he said, 'Proud of you, my boy.'

Tahir could only reply with a smile.

* * *

The elimination of the BYQ gang was a huge setback to the Lashkar-e-Jabbar. When ARQ broke the news to Maulana Asgar, he was furious and immediately asked Maulana Zaif to inquire into it. 'It cannot be possible without a mole within our group,' he said.

The needle of suspicion fell on Ashiq Ahmed and Manzoor Trali in the Kashmir Valley. Maulana Zaif also formed a team of core Lashkar-e-Jabbar cadres to carry out internal surveillance at their Bahawalpur headquarters.

Ismail, the local Lashkar-e-Jabbar commander looking after ground operations in south Kashmir, was given the task of talking to Ashiq and Manzoor. He questioned each of them in detail about the events leading to the deaths of the BYQ gang. Although Manzoor Trali was a senior member of the Lashkar-e-Jabbar, he appeared for questioning, comfortable with the fact that he was not guilty. Ashiq also willingly answered all questions.

After ground verifications of the versions that Ashiq and Manzoor Trali gave, both were given a clean chit by Ismail and the same was conveyed to Maulana Zaif. Ashiq then expressed his desire to become an active cadre of the Lashkar-e-Jabbar in south Kashmir. Ismail accepted his request and held a small swearing-in ceremony, after which Ashiq was handed a new Kalashnikov from the arms dump. However, Ashiq did not survive for long and was killed in a police encounter a month later at Ratnipora in Pulwama.

Chapter 16

Khalid Jutt decided to treat himself, now that he was getting money both from his job at the Lashkar-e-Jabbar HQ and from Atif. On his day off, he visited Bahawalpur Trade Centre, a mall at the heart of the town where one could get readymade garments, shoes and toys at a reasonable price. He bought himself fake Hugo Boss shoes as well as a pair of black Jodhpuri shoes with golden embroidery. He was very fond of watches and bought a 'Made in Dubai' fake Rolex. He then decided to try on some Pathan suits.

When he came out of the trial room wearing a black Pathan suit, Mehjabeen, the girl at the sales counter, looked at him and smiled. 'This one really suits you,' she said.

Khalid needed no more confirmation. He smiled back and looked into the mirror.

Mehjabeen handed him her visiting card while handling his purchase. She said, 'You can come back in a week and exchange it in case you change your mind. Make sure that you don't remove the tag.'

While heading out of the mall, he purchased a small bottle of French perfume from a nearby shop and then went home. At night, he pulled out the Pathan suit to try it on again. While taking it out, the visiting card fell to the ground. Khalid picked it up and read the name, Mehjabeen, meaning 'as beautiful as the moon'. She had really been very pretty, Khalid thought, and decided to go see her again.

The next day, he headed towards the mall again.

'How can I help you, sir?' asked Mehjabeen.

'Nothing, *bas* …' Summoning his courage, he said, 'Do you want to have chai with me at Abdullah bhaijan's stall this evening?'

Mehjabeen smiled back and nodded yes. Abdullah bhaijan's stall was famous for the tea they served. So popular was he at Bahawalpur that the locals called him the king of tea. '*Chai ka sultan, Abdullah bhaijan,*' they used to say.

That evening, they had tea and biscuits from the local bakery and chatted. Khalid described himself as the hostel warden of a local training school. He didn't tell her that they trained the mujahideen there.

Mehjabeen was impressed, not with his calm demeanour, nor with his apparently lavish lifestyle, evident from his shoes and his Rolex watch. She was impressed with his simplicity and the straightforwardness typical of a Jat. They exchanged notes on each other's family backgrounds and left after an hour with a promise to meet every Friday evening at the same place and at the same time.

Khalid reached his room on a high, humming his favourite Atif Aslam song, *Tere Sang Yaara*. Right across his room, ARQ had been given a two-room suite. He was there now, his door open, reading the local newspaper.

Watching Khalid walk into his room, it occurred to ARQ that the boy was dressing in a manner that was not possible with the meagre salary that the Lashkar-e-Jabbar gave him. ARQ made a note of this and went back to reading the newspaper.

* * *

Meanwhile, in Jammu and Kashmir, the government decided to hold the Zilla Development Council (ZDC) elections with a view to decentralize power. The aim was to involve the local residents in the development plans and works of the district. But any election process after the removal of the special status of Jammu and Kashmir was viewed with suspicion. Political parties funded and supported by Pakistan were in a fix. If they refused to participate in the elections, the nationalist parties would have a field day. If they participated in the elections, it would seem like a ratification of the removal of the special status.

The ISI decided that they would call politicians and representatives of political parties supported by them to Dubai to discuss the situation.

Abdullah Veeri of the PDF went along with Rameez Sagar of the State Conference. They were received by Shahid Mir, a prominent Kashmiri businessman based in Dubai, who took them to the Armani Hotel at Burj Khalifa. The stay and expenses were borne by Shahid Mir, who was supported by the ISI. Officers of India's Special Analysis Wing followed him to the Burj Khalifa after which they lost track of him.

Veeri and Sagar were checked into rooms that had an exclusive lift to the corporate suites at Level 123. The ISI had booked a floor at Level 125, where the meeting was scheduled.

The ISI team, headed by Major Hamid Gul, started the conversation. 'They have landed us in a tricky situation,' he said. 'Not taking part in the elections to the ZDC is not a choice we can make. You will have to take part in the elections to see that the other parties do not come to power in the majority of the districts.'

'But what do we do even if we win the elections?' Veeri asked.

'You will be paid for not doing anything,' said Gul.

'What do you mean?' asked Veeri.

'Disrupt each and every session of the ZDC,' he said. 'The idea is to stall every move of the government. Try to pass resolutions condemning the removal of the special status of Jammu and Kashmir. Under no circumstances should you fall into the trap of allocating money for the development of your district. We will take care of all your funds,' said Gul.

'You'll have to instruct the mujahideen in the Valley about this,' said Sagar. 'They have called for a boycott of the elections.'

'Leave the mujahideen to us. They'll do what we tell them,' Gul replied.

The meeting ended with a sumptuous dinner. While parting, a gift bag with a Mont Blanc perfume, pen, wallet and watch was handed to each participant.

'We'll give funds of Rs 50 lakh for each candidate of your party. Anyone who wins the election will get a bonus of another Rs 50 lakh,' said Gul. 'Your regular flow of finances will continue and will be separate from this.'

The guests stayed in the hotel for the night and took the Emirates flight to New Delhi the next morning, and then an Air India flight to Srinagar.

Officers of SAW made note of the movement of Sagar and Veeri at the hotel and at the airport. From the details of the visit to the time and place of their stay to what they had for breakfast to where they'd shopped in Dubai—everything was noted, except what they actually did at the Burj Khalifa.

Back in Karachi, the ISI called for a quick meeting with the mujahideen commanders. Maulana Zaif, Maulana Hafiz of the LeT and Syed Hikmaduddin of Hizbul Tehrir were present. The announcement of the ZDC elections was discussed, and everyone was asked for their opinion as to how to deal with the situation. While Maulana Zaif and Maulana Hafiz proposed the more radical option of attacking multiple locations and multiple targets, especially the candidates of mainstream nationalist parties, Syed Hikmaduddin, who was originally a local Kashmiri, had a different opinion. He proposed that they allow the elections to go on peacefully, and then disrupt ZDC meetings at the district level. He said any violent action before the elections targeting any candidate would discourage candidates of parties who were supported by Pakistan.

Maj. Gul knew that disregarding what Maulana Zaif and Maulana Hafiz had said would have consequences. After all, keeping a bunch of Taliban-trained jihadis in their own backyard for a very long time was fraught with danger. He came up with a middle-path solution, keeping in mind the discussions that had already taken place at the Burj Khalifa.

'We'll let the elections happen, but strike at a major security force target during the election process. We'll avoid any collateral damage to any Kashmiri household,' said Maj. Gul.

Maulana Zaif volunteered for the task. They had the maximum presence of committed mujahideen in the Kashmir Valley, and he knew that Manzoor Trali would help them organize this strike. Maulana Hafiz and Syed Hikmaduddin were asked to stand by and consolidate their position in the Kashmir Valley in terms of hideouts, finances, recruitment and training.

Maulana Zaif returned to Bahawalpur and called ARQ for a meeting. While they were talking, Khalid came in to serve tea and Kashmiri roti. ARQ remained silent till Khalid left the room, surreptitiously signalling to Maulana Zaif to also keep quiet.

When Khalid left, Maulana Zaif raised his eyebrows. 'Why did we need to stop talking?' he asked.

'There's something strange about his behaviour recently,' replied ARQ. 'We need to keep a watch on him and his activities.'

'Get someone to trail him and keep me updated,' said Maulana Zaif.

They resumed talking about the attack Maj. Gul wanted them to carry out. 'We need to carry out such a big attack this time, that everyone will remember it,' ARQ said.

'Yes. Bigger than Budgam,' replied Zaif.

'Inshallah,' replied ARQ. 'We'll use a new group fresh from training at the Mazar-e-Sharief camp for this purpose.

A tunnel that has just been completed in the Hiranagar area can be used this time to send in our men.'

'Send me a list of probable candidates,' said Maulana Zaif. 'And ask Manzoor Trali to arrange for a pickup from Hiranagar, and also to do a reconnaissance of a suitable target, preferably near Jammu. It should be a security force camp.'

ARQ nodded and left. He went to his room and called Saleem, the cleaner at the headquarters, and handed him Rs 5000.

'Follow Khalid Jutt for two days and let me know everything about his movements and whom he meets,' he said. 'In no way should he figure out that he is being trailed.'

After two days, Saleem came back with a report. He detailed Khalid's visit to the mall, his meetings with Mehjabeen at the Abdullah tea stall, his purchases of new clothes, and the visits of his sisters to his room.

ARQ found nothing suspicious in any of these, except the money Khalid seemed to be spending on clothes and eating out. Mujahids were allowed to have girlfriends as long as they followed the Islamic traditions. He gave Saleem another Rs 5000 and asked him to report back if he saw Khalid doing anything suspicious. He need no longer trail him, he said.

* * *

Ismail was in his hideout in the forests above Tral when the message from Maulana Asgar and Zaif reached him. Built underground, the hideout was well camouflaged with the help of wooden logs, which were then covered by a polysheet and leaves. There was one small entry, barely enough to let in one man at a time. There was room inside for five people, and in it was a small stove and rations.

Having received the message, Ismail organized a meeting of Lashkar-e-Jabbar mujahideen along with Manzoor Trali.

Manzoor had a clear plan in his mind. To begin with, he said, a second-hand truck had to be purchased. Usually, the mujahideen would put up a purchaser with fake identity cards and residence proofs so the seller would not know the actual buyer. It was a normal precaution they took to avoid being traced.

Abdul Shakoor, a close supporter of the mujahideen at Tral, who was present at the meeting, spoke up and volunteered to provide one of the trucks he owned. There would be no need to buy a truck now.

Shakoor sent one of his trucks to a workshop owned by Rameez, a cousin of Manzoor Trali, and asked that the chassis number and the engine number be erased. He also prepared three fake number plates. He then went to a police station and lodged a complaint about his truck being stolen. The station house officer recorded the complaint and gave him a receipt.

Meanwhile, Rameez worked on the truck, even changing the colour. The end product was presented after five days of hard work. Shakoor returned to the workshop and was asked to identify his own truck from among the five trucks lined up there. He failed to do so and was so happy with the work that he gave Rameez a sum of rupees one lakh. Rameez politely returned the money, saying, 'This is my bit for the cause of jihad.'

Manzoor Trali messaged Maulana Zaif: 'Vehicle is ready. We are ready for the final attack. We have selected Asif to drive the truck to get the mujahideen from the border at Jammu. Let me know the probable dates.'

'What is the target?' asked Zaif.

'TIA HQ in Srinagar,' Trali wrote. 'The final plan will be decided when the mujahideen reach here. Ismail will keep the IED fabricated. We have enough stock to equip the mujahideen.'

Maulana Zaif called for another meeting at Bahawalpur. Three fidayeen—Umar, Hanif and Shams— were selected to infiltrate this time. So charged was ARQ this time, that he stood up during the meeting and made an emotional speech.

'This is for our brothers who have attained martyrdom. People say that we only organize and push in mujahideen without risking our own lives. I assure you that I am one of you and I have committed my life to the cause of jihad. To prove my point, I volunteer to go in myself with our three brothers. Please take care of my family and of my fellow mujahideen if I am among Allah's chosen ones. *Ameen!*'

'Ameen, ameen!' shouted all present in a chorus. There were murmurs among the mujahideen, discussing this decision of ARQ's.

'He is a true mujahideen.' 'Yes, he is truly one of us.' 'Yes.' 'He leads by example.' 'This is what mujahideens are.' Amid all these comments, Umar hailed the decision saying, 'Qadri sahab!'

All the others replied together in synced chorus: 'Zindabad!'

'Get the tunnel ready and arrange the logistics,' said Maulana Zaif.

They went on to discuss whether they needed to send in weapons with the team. Although they had stocked up enough weapons in the Valley, it was decided that, since it was difficult to arrange material for an IED within Kashmir, they would send ten heavy readymade IEDs along with remote controls. They also decided to send a US-made M-4 rifle with each mujahid. M-4 rifles were a new addition to the mujahideen's arsenal. It was not only more accurate but could also double up as a sniper's rifle. Besides this, they decided to send satellite phones, a spare AK-47 rifle each, and a packet of survival food and medicines.

The next lunar cycle was to start after a week and the second day of the lunar cycle was chosen as the infiltration date—18 November. They checked the weather update on Google, which showed that the day would be bright and sunny, and there was no chance of rain at night.

Manzoor Trali kept checking his mobile phone for messages on Dialog. Suddenly, he received a text on WhatsApp, which he used for his regular contacts who were his *mureed*. The text, in Arabic, was from an unsaved number. He hesitated and then opened the message. In it was a link saying, 'Jihad in Islam'.

It was an interpretation of jihad mentioned in the holy text by Al-Qaeda operatives in Afghanistan. Manzoor Trali looked up the number on Truecaller, and the name 'Aleem Bhai' appeared. Manzoor Trali assumed that it would be Hafiz Aleem, considering the fact that he used to regularly send him such texts. He texted back, asking Aleem to come and meet him after 20 November.

At the Crime Branch headquarters, Rajveer's tech team was ecstatic.

One click on the dummy link sent by the TIA compromised the phone of Manzoor Trali. They had successfully infiltrated Manzoor Trali's cell phone, whose Dialog application had been active during the Ban toll plaza encounter. At that time, a team had been assigned the task of continuously monitoring the data thrown up by his cell phone. The team included one person who was Kashmiri and who knew Arabic.

On 14 November, a Dialog message flashed on Manzoor Trali's phone: '*Baraat 18 November ko niklegi, Shalimar banquet hall mein milenge.*' [The marriage party will leave on 18 November. Will meet at Shalimar banquet hall.]

Rajveer saw the message and immediately deciphered it: Fidayeens would infiltrate on 18 November. The meeting point was Samba Bein Highway, through the Samba border.

He got two teams readied immediately: one to handle round-the-clock surveillance on Manzoor Trali, and the other to be at the Samba border on 18 November.

While driving back home in the evening, he thought to himself: '*Manzoor Trali is bigger than what we think. He gave us a small bit of information regarding the meeting in Afghanistan, which would not have led to anything for us if it had not been for our contact with Atif Yusufzai. In fact, he appears to be deeply involved in the Lashkar-e-Jabbar's operations.*'

Chapter 17

The ZDC elections took place in October 2020. The PDF and the State Conference won most of the seats in the Kashmir Valley. The ISI congratulated Abdullah Veeri and Rameez Sagar and a sum of Rs 1 crore was sent across to them through the hawala channel. They were asked to ensure that regular meetings of the allied elected members took place, and to devise a strategy whereby problematic issues would be raised in each session that would put the administration on the back foot and give a reason for the separatists to come out on to the streets.

As a first step, the ISI handlers asked them for a list of the non-PDF and State Conference candidates who had won. ISI instructed the till-then-dormant outfit of Syed Hikmaduddin to activate pistol-holding cadres to target and eliminate these candidates.

One of them was Rahul Pandit, the lone member of the Pandit community to have won in the ZDC elections. He had not left his apple orchards at Shopian even when terror activity was peaking in the area. There were times when

the local Muslims would find out about the movement of
terrorists in that area and would invite Rahul Pandit and
his family into their homes to keep them safe. He would
take part in all the religious and social celebrations of
the Muslim community, and this was reciprocated by the
Muslims during Hindu festivals. Not surprisingly, when he
stood for the ZDC elections, he had overwhelming support
and was elected as a ZDC member from his constituency.
Confident of the support, love and affection that he got
from his village, he refused security even when it was
offered to him.

On the morning of 14 November 2020, he set out of
his house to make the traditional *gharaunda* (a miniature
house made out of bricks and clay) for his children on the
occasion of Diwali. He collected soft clay from a nearby field
and then went to the kiln to get some bricks to make the
gharaunda. As soon as he reached the kiln, a local terrorist,
Imtiaz from Kulgam, came up from behind and shot him
in the head, killing him on the spot. The Hizbul Tehrir,
led by Maulana Hikmaduddin, claimed responsibility for
the attack. Imtiaz, a new recruit to the organization, had
carried out his first-ever attack and was rewarded for it
with a promotion to being an AK-47-wielding mujahid.
He would now be a part of bigger attacks in the future.

* * *

It was a quiet day at the Lashkar-e-Jabbar headquarters in
Bahawalpur. The Friday namaz was offered by everyone
together, including Maulana Asgar, and he used the time
to give fiery speeches against India on the Kashmir issue.

After the namaz, Khalid returned to his room, put on his favourite Pathan suit and Jodhpuri shoes, sprayed himself generously with perfume and set out for the Abdullah tea stall.

Excited about meeting his girlfriend, he had rushed out of the room, leaving his phone behind. Saleem, who had been keeping an eye on him, took the opportunity to enter his room and check his belongings. There was nothing unusual: just clothes, a few hundred Pakistani rupees in the pocket of his shirt, and Mehjabeen's visiting card. Just as Saleem was about to leave the room, Khalid's phone rang. Saleem looked at the mobile and saw that it was an Echochat call from someone called 'Alif ye'.

Unusual name, Saleem thought. He was smart enough not to answer the call.

He immediately went to ARQ and told him about the call. *Why should he use the Echochat app,* ARQ wondered. Although the app was a favoured mode of communication for the mujahids, it was only used by the active cadres, not by those who worked on normal office chores. Since ARQ was already suspicious of Khalid, he started putting two and two together. He immediately called for the technical team to have a look at the mobile phone. It was the latest model of an Android phone from which data extraction was not particularly easy. The tech team finally advised against any tampering with the phone and suggested that they bug his room instead.

ARQ immediately instructed Saleem to go to Abdullah's tea stall and keep a watch on Khalid. Saleem got on his motorcycle and headed quickly to the tea stall. By the time he reached, Khalid and Mehjabeen had finished their tea and snacks and were saying goodbye to each other. Saleem called up ARQ and informed him that Khalid would most likely be home in half an hour. ARQ realized that they wouldn't have enough time to bug the room properly, so he postponed the plan till the next Friday.

Khalid had cut short the time he had with Mehjabeen because he was uncomfortable about having left his mobile in his room. He skipped the usual stroll they took after tea, saying there was an important meeting at the hostel. He returned to his room and was relieved to see his mobile in the same place that he had left it. He unlocked his mobile and there was a missed call from 'Alif Ye'. *Atif Yusufzai*, he murmured and then opened the app to see if there were any messages. 'Call. Urgent', was the message from Atif.

Khalid locked his room from the inside and made the call.

'Is there a new group going to India from Shakargarh?' asked Atif.

'I have no idea,' replied Khalid.

'Can you try and find out about this?' asked Atif.

'Yes. Is it urgent?' Khalid asked.

'Yes. I need a revert within two days,' replied Atif.

Khalid had never asked a direct question regarding the activities of the Lashkar-e-Jabbar and was hesitant to do so now. The next morning, he went to ARQ and expressed his willingness to work actively for the cause of the Lashkar-e-Jabbar.

'I am in awe of those who are willing to commit themselves to jihad. I can assure you that no fighter in the

Lashkar-e-Jabbar can match me in terms of courage. Give me a chance to prove myself,' said Khalid.

ARQ was taken by surprise. Since he had started working at the Lashkar-e-Jabbar office, he had seen that Khalid was content with what he was doing and happy that he got time to take care of his sisters and mother at home. '*What could be the reason for this change?*' ARQ wondered.

'Are you willing to be a part of the next movement of our jihadis?' asked ARQ.

'Any time,' replied Khalid. He was hoping to get the reply that would serve his purpose. 'Is there a group going soon?' he asked.

ARQ did not want to disclose any details to Khalid, so he just shook his head.

'It's not an easy thing to do. It requires a lot of planning, preparation and motivation. You will have to attend sessions on Islam with Qari sahab before we find you fit for jihad,' said ARQ. He continued, 'I need you to do something for me. Go to Lodhran and tell Qari sahab to come to Bahawalpur from next week onwards to take regular classes on Islam. He is an old man and has a special aversion towards mobile phones.' He knew that the journey would take Khalid at least three hours.

Like an obedient soldier, Khalid went to the bus stand and waited for a bus to Lodhran. It arrived after fifteen minutes; he boarded it and left.

The tech team of ARQ immediately entered Khalid's room and started to place bugs in it. One behind the picture of Mohammed Ali Jinnah and one near the wooden ceiling rafters. They needed to place the highly sensitive audio receptors in such a way that they could capture each word uttered in any corner of the room.

'It's all done,' said the head of the tech team after two hours.

The listening station was placed in a room in the basement of the office complex, in one corner of the parking lot. Residents of the complex assumed that it was a storeroom; very few knew that behind a wooden panel on one wall, there was another small room. Entry was limited to those whose irises had been scanned and fed in earlier. Maulana Asgar, Zaif and ARQ were the only ones allowed in, besides a tech team comprising five people who had been carefully chosen. They were veterans who had been in the Kashmir Valley earlier and had returned after the successful completion of their tenure.

To test the bugs, Saleem went to the room, closed the door and made a sound from each corner. He then lay down on the bed and whispered a few sentences. The tech team gave a thumbs-up: they could hear every word clearly.

'Don't forget to ensure that the power backup of the monitoring room is functioning properly,' ARQ reminded them.

Khalid delivered the message at Lodhran to Qari sahab and returned after four hours, exhausted. He headed straight to the canteen and had his favourite butter chicken and rice.

Soon after, he went to ARQ's room. 'Qari sahab says he will come from next week,' said Khalid.

During the half-hour interaction with Qari sahab, Khalid had been impressed with his knowledge of Islam and the manner in which he explained verses from the Quran to students who had gathered there. He had enjoyed the session so much, Khalid was tempted to actually join the movement and cross over to India with the other jihadis. As per Qari sahab, jihad was not only lawful as per Islam but also a duty cast upon every individual. Khalid had not developed an interest in Islam while training at Herat, but he had listened to every word uttered by Qari sahab, such was the latter's way of presentation. He saw the logic in what he was saying. No wonder he was the chief preacher for the Lashkar-e-Jabbar in Bahawalpur.

When Khalid returned to his room, he texted Atif Yusufzai.

'Call me when you are free,' he wrote.

He then called Mehjabeen and spoke to her for a while. From a vacation to Mangla Dam at Mirpur to a probable wedding date to having five children, three boys and two girls—they discussed it all. He then called his sisters and mother. When his mother expressed concern about the finances for the marriage of his eldest sister, Khalid replied, 'Leave it to me.'

'When will you come home?' his mother asked.

'When the training is over,' he replied

They then discussed other things, including how pious Khalid's father had been and how he had suddenly left for his heavenly abode.

Listening in the monitoring room, Saleem was emotional and his eyes became moist. '*Should we be listening to our own men?*' he asked himself.

Once Khalid had fallen asleep, the tech team put the system on recording mode and retired for the night.

Early the next morning, after the Fajr namaz, Khalid's mobile phone rang. It was Atif Yusufzai. Khalid ensured his room was locked and then picked up the phone.

'Did you find out about when the movement will take place?' asked Atif.

'I tried, but there was no certain reply,' replied Khalid. 'ARQ asked me if I was willing to join the jihadis in the next batch,' he continued.

With a view to secure the future of his mother and sisters, Khalid considered striking a deal with Atif Yusufzai before he actually joined the jihadis.

'I need some money for my family. They are in need of it,' said Khalid. He asked Atif for 50 lakh Pakistani rupees for his family and promised to get the exact information about the movement of the current batch from Shakargarh. Atif was sure that he could bill this to Maneesh without too many questions being asked. He told Khalid that he would ensure the money reached his family that very same day,

Khalid hung up the phone and went out to speak to ARQ. He looked all over for him but could not find him.

In the basement, ARQ walked into the monitoring room and asked his team to replay the recordings from the previous night. From 10 p.m. to around 5 a.m. the noise graph on the screen was flat, except for minor fluctuations arising from the noise that the fan made, and one major fluctuation at 2 a.m., when Khalid woke up to go to the washroom.

There was another major fluctuation for about five minutes after the Fajr namaz. ARQ asked the team to play the recording again. And then again.

'*Khalid is definitely talking to the enemy,*' he said to himself. He nodded to his team and headed out to discuss the matter with Maulana Zaif. On the way, he was stopped by Khalid, who said he wanted to discuss something important.

'I have made up my mind to join jihad,' said Khalid.

'Why such a change of heart?' asked ARQ.

'I listened to Qari sahab and liked his discourse. I am now convinced that this is the right path for me,' said Khalid. 'Can I join the next group?'

'Not until your compulsory three-month course on Islam is complete,' said ARQ.

'Is the next batch going in before that?' asked Khalid.

'We're not sure yet,' ARQ said and walked away.

He headed to Maulana Zaif's office and told him he was convinced that Khalid was the mole in their camp. He called for a copy of the recordings and played the relevant portions to Maulana Zaif. He also described their recent conversations.

Maulana Zaif called his brother Maulana Asgar in, and in a closed-door meeting, they went over and analysed Khalid Jutt's every movement. Each one presented instances when they observed an anomaly in his behaviour. Maulana Zaif remembered that Khalid had been present, serving food, at the time when the details of the movement of the BYQ gang were being discussed.

The meeting ended with a fatwa against Khalid, which Maulana Asgar had the authority to issue. Khalid would be indicted and executed for treason and for being responsible for the death of three mujahideen. ARQ was tasked with the responsibility of questioning Khalid to get the details of his handlers before he was executed.

Saleem was outside the room, waiting to be called in to clean up, and he overheard a furious Maulana Asgar ordering ARQ to teach Khalid a lesson. Saleem had developed a soft corner for Khalid after hearing his conversation with his mother and sisters. Caught between his commitment towards the Lashkar-e-Jabbar and his sympathy for Khalid, he finally decided to warn Khalid. He quickly went to Khalid's room and told him what he had overheard. He advised him to leave Bahawalpur immediately.

Khalid was scared. He knew that the Lashkar-e-Jabbar was ruthless and their method of punishment was nothing less than beheading. As soon as Saleem left, he pulled out his phone and called Atif Yusufzai. 'Maulana is suspicious of me and has asked someone to question me,' he said.

'How do you know?' asked Atif Yusufzai.

'Saleem informed me. I am leaving the Bahawalpur camp immediately,' said Khalid.

Before Atif could ask any more questions, Khalid hung up. He grabbed whatever cash he had and his identity card and left the building. He didn't want to waste time packing the rest of his belongings.

Atif Yusufzai was concerned. Even if Khalid was somehow able to withstand interrogation and did not reveal his identity when questioned, Atif was the one who had recommended that Khalid be kept at the headquarters at Bahawalpur. And if the Lashkar-e-Jabbar complained to the Taliban, he would meet the same fate as Khalid. He took a quick decision. Before the Lashkar-e-Jabbar got hold of Khalid, he needed to get him eliminated. He immediately called Gul Mohammed, a mercenary that he knew he could rely on, and gave him instructions as well as Khalid's address. Knowing Khalid, Atif felt sure that he would never disappear before first meeting his family.

Gul Mohammed immediately headed to Khalid's village and began surveillance of his house.

Khalid arrived late at night, after a twelve-hour journey from Bahawalpur by the state roadways bus. His family was surprised and happy to see him.

'Why are you here so late?' asked his sister, Albeena.

'I'm on official work here for a short period,' he replied.

Albeena offered him some food, which he had. Khalid knew that he did not have much time before the Lashkar-e-Jabbar landed up. He barely got any sleep, constantly watching outside for any signs of movement. Early the next morning, he had breakfast with his mother and sisters and then told them that he needed to leave to get his work done. He promised to be back by the evening and left behind his bag, which had cash and his identity card.

Outside his house, he decided to meet Mehjabeen for one last time. He calculated the time a taxi would take to reach Bahawalpur and guessed that he could be there by 6 p.m. He took a Cabcall taxi and proceeded to Bahawalpur. On the way, Khalid called Mehjabeen and asked her to be at the Abdulla tea stall at 6 p.m. He then switched off his mobile and slept, little aware that two men on a motorcycle were following him.

Mehjabeen was already at the tea stall when Khalid got there. They had their usual tea and Khalid ordered aloo parathas for both of them. Afterwards, they walked towards the Lahore High Court complex, which was a secluded area in which they could have some privacy. As they walked, Khalid told her that he was going away for a few weeks. He said that on his return he would meet her parents to ask for Mehjabeen's hand in marriage. Mehjabeen was ecstatic and took hold of his hand, looking around to make sure no one would see the gesture. When she looked back, she saw a motorcycle speeding towards them. She immediately let go of his hand, lowered her burqa and stepped a little away from Khalid.

Khalid looked back, curious as to what she had seen. The motorcycle came close to them. So close that it almost grazed Khalid. As it went past him, the pillion rider fired two shots at Khalid's head, and the motorcycle sped away.

Khalid collapsed to the ground, blood oozing out of his head, while a shocked Mehjabeen fell to her knees next to him, shouting for help.

In Kabul, Atif Yusufzai received a message, informing him that the job was done. He heaved a sigh of relief.

Meanwhile, the Lashkar-e-Jabbar team dispatched by ARQ had reached Khalid's house at Gujranwala three hours after he had left. Khalid's family passed on what they had been told—that he had left on official work. Having obtained Khalid's call data through their contacts in the ISI, they reached out to Mehjabeen—the last call made by Khalid. A sobbing Mehjabeen informed them about what had happened, and that the local police were on the spot, to investigate the murder.

The team passed on the information to ARQ, who decided to let things lie for the time being. The informant had been killed—by whom, they could try and find out later. Right now, he had a mission to focus on.

Chapter 18

Abdul Rehman Qadri took leave for a day on 15 November and went to his home in Muzaffargarh, which was a three-hour drive away. He spent time with his wife and children, and then called each one of his relatives and asked about their well-being. Later in the afternoon, he played cricket with his children, Arsh and Waqar, in the nearby fields and returned exhausted but happy. Safeena was meeting her husband after a long time, and while he was playing cricket with the children, she rushed to a nearby beauty parlour. They had decided to have at least four children when they got married, and it was time they made efforts to have another baby, she thought.

When the children were outside playing with friends, Safeena and ARQ went to their room. She was indeed beautiful, he thought, with large brown eyes and a well-maintained body. The fragrance of the beauty products freshly applied at the parlour was enticing. Visiting his home after a month, ARQ would usually have wasted no time making love. However, on this day, he sat down on the bed and made Safeena sit beside him. Safeena saw that his general demeanour was very different. He took her face in his hands, like he would of a beloved sibling, and kissed her forehead. Then he took a paper from his pocket and read it out to Safeena. A bank account in Pakistan State Bank with a balance of Rs 27,00,000, a piece of 20 kanals (a measurement of land, approximately 5000 sq. ft) of agricultural land at Shujabaad, a flat at Bahawalpur, fixed deposits and a life insurance certificate.

Safeena was no fool. She had been married to ARQ long enough to sense what was going on. They *had* planned four children, but the first oath they had taken together at the mosque after their marriage was fixed was to commit their lives to the cause of jihad. She remembered the oath now.

At night, Safeena made ARQ his favourite makki di roti and sarson da saag for dinner, with two dollops of homemade butter and a helping of jaggery. Though he had not eaten anything for hours, ARQ did not have much appetite.

After the pretence of dinner, he went with Safeena to the room where their children were studying. ARQ tried to teach social studies to Arsh but closed the book after ten minutes. His mind was continuously occupied with different thoughts and he just could not concentrate on anything specific.

The children were sent to bed early that night and ARQ and Safeena retired to their bedroom. They spent a lot of time talking to each other. Sometime after 1 a.m., Safeena drifted off to sleep, but ARQ continued to stare at the ceiling, lost in his tsunami of thoughts. *How would they achieve the mission? Would Allah give him a place in heaven?*

Would Arsh become a pilot? Would Waqar be able to join the army? Who was the best person to take care of the family in his absence? Would he be able to return home after his stint in Kashmir? The last question haunted him particularly, even though he knew that Safeena was a strong woman, as committed to jihad as he was, and capable of taking care of the family on her own.

At 5 a.m., ARQ finally left his bed, did his *wudu* (ritual cleansing in Islam) and sat down for Fajr namaz. He then went to the room where his children were sleeping and kissed them gently, taking care that he did not wake them up. He then silently went up to his wife, who was preparing breakfast. He reached out and switched the gas off and took her to their room. They sat in silence for a while. After a few minutes, they hugged each other and cried for what seemed like a lifetime.

The sense of humour of time is classic! When you have limited time and you wish it to go slowly, somehow time gets to know and it moves quickly. Before they knew it, ARQ had to leave. Safeena handed him a tabeej made by the local maulvi for his safety and ARQ got into the cab that was waiting for him. He was a man on a mission, now, and leaving with a clear purpose in his mind. The mission required no baggage, no bedding, no change of clothes, no packed food. Everything was taken care of when a mujahid set out for jihad. The ISI funded them lavishly for participating in the task. In fact, all those setting out from Pakistan towards Kashmir were taken to the local army canteen at Bahawalpur, where they were allowed to shop for whatever they wanted. When ARQ was taken there, he had picked up a set of binoculars, a powerful small torch on which he later had his name engraved, a camouflage jacket and a black and grey Munib Nawaz salwar kameez set. On the way out, he took three packets of Bateel Ajwa dates, which he was very fond of.

He reached the Bahawalpur headquarters by noon and went straight to his room. After taking a shower, he met Maulana Asgar and Maulana Zaif. They spent three hours discussing the plan in detail. Umar, Hanief and Shams were called in towards the end of the meeting and asked to get ready. They packed their favourite clothes, eatables and other belongings in rucksacks and went for the Maghrib namaz together. ARQ accompanied them as the head of the squad.

They then went to the barracks at Bahawalpur, where everyone had assembled for the final ceremonies that the Lashkar-e-Jabbar followed before any special task. The leadership avoided attending this ritual since the fidayeens let loose on the occasion, singing and dancing, which was against the Deobandi school of thought of the Lashkar-e-Jabbar.

Hanief grabbed the microphone and sang:

Nabi ke sahaba ke raste pe chalke; [moving on the path of the Prophet]

Dilon ka sukoon hum ne haasil kiya hai; [I have attained peace at heart]

Laga hai nasha jab se Jannat ka humko; [since the time I have been thinking about the heavens]

Uchaat apna jee is Jahan se hua hai; [I have got fed up of the life on earth]

Mahazon se aati hai Jannat ki Khushboo; [in suffering I get the fragrance of heavens]

Mere dil ko bechain kiye ja rahi hai [it keeps troubling my heart]

The song was a favourite among the Lashkar-e-Jabbar suicide attackers, who felt that going to Kashmir was like heading to the battlefield and had been told that seventy-two *hoors* (fairies) awaited them in heaven.

They then played a traditional game of guess and flog. Two boys were blindfolded and had to hold on to a centrepiece with one hand while moving around and trying to flog the other boy with the other hand with a thick rope made out of cloth. The one who flogged the other more accurately won the game. Umar and Shams played while the others watched. Umar won and was awarded an extra helping of fried chicken for dinner.

Shams had to undergo the penalty, which was that he was dressed like a woman, blindfolded and made to move around the room, trying to kick the others. All the mujahids enjoyed the game, breaking into laughter every time Shams missed the target.

After the traditional games, they all sat down for a feast. A long piece of white cloth was rolled out in the centre of the carpet, and food was laid out on it. All the members sat in a circle and Saleem, who had been upgraded to the post of cook, served them dinner, which comprised roasted fish, chicken fry, mutton rogan josh, Hyderabadi biryani and tandoori roti, ending with phirni for dessert.

* * *

It was 5 a.m. and Rajveer had decided to jog on the streets of Jammu instead of going to the gym. He felt the need for fresh air to keep his mind alert and focused. He wanted nothing more than to get to the root of the Lashkar-e-Jabbar and defeat them once and for all. Meanwhile, he also had his personal life occupying his mind. On the one hand, he felt that his teenage children needed him around more. On the other, his father had not been keeping too well lately. He and Nikita had spoken and decided that they needed to get him to Delhi for a check-up soon, both of them knowing fully well that the end may be near sooner than later. It was painful to see his father go through these health issues.

After breakfast with his parents, he left for the office, a man on a mission with a clear purpose in mind.

It had been another busy day at work and before he knew it, it was evening. He was standing by his office window, looking out and thinking of nothing in particular. Just then, a message appeared on his phone. 'Long time ...', followed by a smiley emoji.

Rajveer was taken aback. Why was Mehak texting after such a long gap?

'Yes, long time. How have you been?' he replied, feeling pleased at the thought of being remembered. He held on to his phone, waiting for the message.

'Nothing interesting since I joined the security wing. Just the routine, monotonous duties of VIP security. I texted because I thought of you.'

He paused for a moment before he replied. 'That's the difference, I never stopped thinking of you ...' He had always been good with words.

She replied with another smiley emoji. While he was wondering what to write next, his phone pinged. He looked at it expectantly. It was from Nikita. 'Have spoken to the doctor. His advice is not to relocate Papa. His condition is not good enough for that. He said it's best to keep him there.'

As he was reading it, another message popped up. 'Want to meet?' From Mehak. There were such mixed thoughts in his mind, he couldn't figure out what to say or do.

'Is it still a question in your mind?' was his reply to Mehak.

His phone began to ring. *Tum se mil ke … aisa laga …*

'Haan?' he said without any pleasantries.

'It's best to keep him there. He will not be able to handle the relocation, the doctor said,' said Nikita

'Yes, I read your message. If that is the doctor's final decision, then we have little choice in the matter. We'll have him stay here and pray for the best.' There was a sense of finality in his voice. The tone of his voice said that he was not really interested in speaking any further. They ended their conversation.

He had some mixed thoughts in his mind when his phone pinged. 'Yes, it's still a question because I have put on a lot of weight and you may not want to see me.'

'You … and put on weight? Is that even possible? I will need to pick you up to check if you have put on weight.' He ended his message with a wink emoji.

His thoughts went back to his father and his condition. How he wished that he could solve the issue and make it easier for him.

'I'll text soon. It's 16 November today, I will message you soon.'

* * *

At 10 p.m. after dinner on 16 November, the four fidayeens—ARQ, Shams, Hanief and Umar—emerged out of the barracks carrying their rucksacks. Accompanied by a barber, Rameez, an armourer, Haseeb, and a cook, Suleman, they boarded a luxury Coaster Saloon bus which would transport them to Shakargarh.

The fidayeen squad arrived in Shakargarh at 11 the next morning, after having halted at Lahore for tea and a short nap of four hours. They headed straight to the Lashkar-e-Jabbar transit camp and dozed off there. In the evening, they were taken to the stock room to pick up their kit. Each of them received a rucksack with a pre-assembled IED vest and a remote control triggering device. The Lashkar-e-Jabbar always had a fallback system in case a fidayeen developed cold feet at the last minute. They also carried an AK-47 rifle with four magazines each, six grenades, a matrix sheet for communication, one I-Com set each, a GPS device, light sleeping bags, an M-4 rifle with night sight, one pistol each and two light machine guns between them.

Back at the camp, an ISI member taught them how to use the matrix sheets. Some quick messages required just one column to be read out. For example, 'We have crossed' was set as AB on the matrix sheet, whereas 'We have been received' was reflected as BD on the matrix sheet. Their I-Com sets were kept on the charger and each had a spare battery. They were also given a briefing using a Google map projected on a big screen, where the route to be taken was explained. The briefing also included the coordinates of the tunnel, the exit, the BSF posts in the vicinity, and the route to be followed up to the highway and the subsequent journey to the target location. A dhaba on the national highway, run by an overground worker of the Lashkar-e-Jabbar, was fixed as the refreshment point. The dhaba owner, Nadeem, was famous for his rajma–chawal, and the place was always crowded with visitors. He used the rush to camouflage the movement of terrorists on the highway.

After the briefing, the squad had a quiet dinner and retreated to sleep early.

* * *

'Let's meet at the Cave-in Café. It's not too crowded and we'll get a chance to catch up.'

'Time?' replied Rajveer.

'2000 hours,' was Mehak's reply.

Though he had responded eagerly when she had messaged earlier, Rajveer had realized in the intervening days that he did not want to indulge in anything like this. He remembered reading, 'A man has only enough blood to operate his brain or his penis at a time. Somehow both don't seem to work together.' He smiled to himself—suddenly the statement seemed to be coming true. Looked like all the blood was in the brain now.

As always, Mehak looked gorgeous. Any man would give his right arm and a leg to be with her in private, Rajveer thought. Yet, he was in a different zone, and his blood was clearly operating only his brain. Mehak could sense this immediately. This was not what she had expected, and somewhere in the back of her mind, she felt rejected.

Casually, she gently brushed her hand against his in the hope of some reaction. Rajveer was no fool and was quick to pick up the hint, but there was just too much happening on his personal and professional front; he didn't want to complicate things on either front. The Mehak chapter had closed some years ago, he realized, and he wanted to keep it like that. Though the man inside him urged him to take a step in that direction, the family man in him prevented him from doing so.

He gave her a sweet, genuine smile and began, 'This last year has been—'

She interrupted him, saying, 'You know, the best thing about you is … your smile.'

He felt his resolve weaken.

She continued, 'And, there are three reasons why you must smile.' When he looked at her questioningly, she said, 'First, it increases your face value. Second, you look best when you smile and third …' She paused dramatically and held his hand gently before she continued, 'And the third, you never know who is falling in love with your smile!' She smiled broadly and gently squeezed his hand.

Rajveer felt smitten by her beauty and words again. His blood seemed to be going from his brain to other parts of his body.

Just then, his phone rang. Looking at the number on the screen, his blood gushed back to his brain. He answered the call and said, 'Yes?' He listened for about thirty seconds and then hung up.

He placed a gentle hand on Mehak's arm and said in the most polite manner he knew, 'I have to rush. We will have a nice, quiet dinner some other day.' He got up, knowing that Mehak would understand. She understood the call of duty, and somewhere inside, her heart would pardon him. She would also know inside the same heart that whatever there was between them so many years ago was certainly not there any more. There was not going to be a quiet dinner between them, ever. It was over.

Chapter 19

The next morning, 18 November, the fidayeen squad was taken to a nearby field for firing practice. They took turns firing the light machine gun, the M-4 rifle, the AK-47 and the pistol. The villagers gathered at a distance, watching them practise and laugh at each other, making fun of poor range drills. The squad then moved towards the border, a guide leading them. They reached the border by around noon. The area had dense bushes and a generous growth of elephant grass, which the Pakistani rangers never bothered to cut. It provided them with good camouflage for any covert activity along the border.

ARQ reached out to the Pakistani ranger post along the border and stated a code. He was immediately allowed in to see the captain in charge of the border post. After accepting a cup of tea, ARQ explained the plan to the captain, who listened carefully and then described the tactical movement they would have to adopt before entering the tunnel. They would have to move at night, bending and crawling as they approached the tunnel since it was close to the border and they could be spotted, and maintaining a distance of at least five metres between themselves to minimize casualties in case there was firing from across the border. The captain would play a role only if there was trouble and if the fidayeens needed cover fire to retreat.

ARQ returned to the rest of the men after half an hour. They then moved closer to the mouth of the tunnel. At this time, ARQ opened up his Q-mobile and messaged Manzoor Trali on Dialog: *'Aaj shaadi hogi.'*

Manzoor Trali was already at Samba, loading Shakoor's truck with Zamindaara basmati rice bags to be taken to Awantipora. Though it had been decided earlier that Asif would drive the mujahids to Tral, Manzoor had decided to take on the task himself, considering how important the plan was to the Lashkar-e-Jabbar. He glanced at his watch; it showed 1 p.m. Based on his experience, he guessed that infiltration would most likely be at midnight. By his calculations, it would take them another three hours to travel around 10 km, walking along the rivulet to reach the highway. So he would have till at least 2 a.m. to reach the national highway at Samba. He asked his helper, Waseem, to create a cavity inside the truck, where at least four people and their baggage could be housed.

***

Rajveer's team was excited. They passed on the text message to Trali's phone to the sub-team already carrying out surveillance on him. Meanwhile, considering the importance of the operation, the DIG and SSP Jammu were told about the situation on a specially secured lease line. Two teams were formed: one to follow Manzoor Trali and the other to intercept ARQ and his team at a suitable location. The interception team selected Nagrota as the best place for interception for various reasons including the fact that it was a fairly secluded area, so collateral damage would be avoided. Police commandos were placed at strategic locations at Nagrota as well as a command vehicle which had pan-tilt-zoom (PTZ) cameras and a control room inside, from where the operation could be controlled. Two cut-off parties were placed a kilometre behind the earmarked place, to make sure that no civilian vehicle moved towards them once the terrorists were intercepted. Drones were kept ready inside the command vehicle, to be used in case the terrorists escaped in the nearby ravines. The newly acquired drones also had a system whereby announcements could be made, which could prove handy if they wanted to say something to the terrorists. They also had a thermal imager, which could be used to spot terrorists in the dark.

* * *

ARQ and his team had lunch, which had been made for them at Shakargarh. The roti, kheema mutter and mutton stew were heated on the portable gas stove which they had carried with them. There was also milk, poured into a Mountain Dew bottle. They each had a sip, one by one, all drinking from the same bottle. While eating, they fed each other out of affection.

It was now the turn of Rameez, the barber, to give them the customary shave. Haseeb, the armourer, had a final look at the weapons they were carrying. He disassembled each weapon and gave one final pull-through on each barrel to make sure that everything was in working condition.

Haseeb had also been given the task of carrying back all the oxygen cylinders once they exited the tunnel on the Indian side.

After everything was done, ARQ briefed the others regarding the movement pattern, precautions to be taken while moving, who would handle the GPS device, who would respond to the secret code at the roadhead, and what was to be done in case of a firefight.

By this time, it was nearing last light, and they performed namaz together. They then took pictures and selfies on their mobile phones before it got too dark, pulled out their sleeping bags and rested before embarking on what they knew would be a full night's work. ARQ took a selfie lying inside his sleeping bag and sent it to his wife. This was against the code of the Lashkar-e-Jabbar, but ARQ felt he could violate it, being the seniormost at the moment. They had five hours to go before they entered the tunnel.

*   *   *

After Waseem had created the cavity inside the truck, Manzoor sent him out to get four packets of biryani with mutton stew from a nearby dhaba for the visitors. While Waseem was away, Manzoor received another message on his Dialog app. It just mentioned 'Dogra', followed by two six-digit alphabetical codes, AQRBHI and GFTWAR, mentioning the latitude and longitude of the rendezvous point. Manzoor understood that Dogra was the code that he had to cite while picking up the mujahideen.

Rajveer's team was confused by the code and could not decipher it. They put a couple of people on it; the number of letters seemed to indicate that it was a latitude and longitude that had been provided.

* * *

Waseem returned at 10 p.m. with the food and Manzoor Trali asked him to place it inside the cavity in the truck. He then told Waseem to rest inside the godown, saying he would let him know if he needed anything. A shrewd man, Manzoor Trali never disclosed the whole plan to anyone, not even his close associates. Manzoor boarded the truck and tried to sleep for a couple of hours inside the driver's cabin. When it was 1 a.m., he started the truck and drove towards Samba.

Manzoor switched on the music system as he drove. A Kashmiri tune came on. Ironically, the one-liner at the back of the truck read, 'Death Keeps No Calendar'.

* * *

While Manzoor was at the loading yard, the sub-team had quietly slipped a tiny GPS tracker in a bag of rice in one corner, just in case they lost track of the vehicle. It only required a small slit in the bag for the GPS tracker to be pushed in. Another device that was slipped in was a sophisticated high-sensor microphone which had a battery life of twenty-four hours and could pick up the weakest of noises. So, any communication could be heard by the team following in another vehicle at a distance.

* * *

ARQ and his team entered the tunnel at midnight and exited after twenty minutes. Again, the end of the tunnel

was amid dense bushes. Shams was the first one to get out.
He looked all around and saw the lighting on the border
fence barely 100 yards from them. There was a BSF picket
looking towards the Pakistani side. Once he was sure that
everything was safe, he signalled to his colleagues to come
out. First Hanief, then Umar and then ARQ. Haseeb
turned back with the extra baggage. Hanief then covered
the mouth of the tunnel with the sandbags they'd brought
with them, and then placed twigs and leaves over it.

Shams opened the Garmin set and followed the pre-
mapped route carefully, hiding it inside his jacket so the
light from the GPS device would not be noticed. Hanief,
Umar and ARQ followed him, maintaining a distance
of about twenty yards from each other. Once they were
at a sufficient distance from the BSF deployment, their
movements became more relaxed and they used the light
of their mobile phones to avoid obstacles. They walked for
three hours, taking water breaks after every half hour, and
finally reached the roadhead on the national highway at
3.15 a.m. at the pre-decided GPS location. They could see
a truck parked at a distance of about 50 metres. The given
GPS location was under a bridge, which had sufficient
undergrowth to provide a hiding place. ARQ and his team
waited under the bridge for some time and rested.

After ten minutes, they heard calls of 'Dogra, dogra'.
ARQ indicated to his team to remain quiet and not respond.
They were taught to take this precaution during training.
The drill was to observe the movement after the receiver
made the first call just in case he had been apprehended
and was under the control of the forces. Manzoor Trali kept
walking in the same direction to ensure that no one noticed

anything unusual in his movements. He went to one side and relieved himself. He then turned around, reached the given rendezvous point and again whispered, 'Dogra.' This time Hanief walked out and approached Manzoor Trali.

'*As salaam alaikum*,' he said.

'*Walekum as salaam*,' replied Manzoor Trali and then asked in Kashmiri, 'Are you fine?'

Manzoor knew well that the mujahideen would not know Kashmiri and had asked this expecting a certain reply.

'Speak in Urdu,' replied Hanief.

'Where are the rest?' asked Manzoor.

'Everyone is here,' replied Hanief.

Manzoor opened the side door of the truck, which led straight to the cavity between the bags of rice, and asked Hanief to get the others in quickly.

'*Pehle bhaijaan japphi toh pao* [first give me a hug],' Hanief said.

Manzoor hugged Hanief, and while he did so, Hanief frisked Manzoor for any weapon he might be carrying. He did this so subtly, Manzoor did not realize he was being frisked. It is said that terrorists don't even trust their own fathers when it comes to matters related to jihad. Manzoor could sense the other's suspicion but kept quiet. He himself had felt the same way many times while working for the Lashkar-e-Jabbar, which was the reason he was one of the longest-surviving terrorists in the Kashmir Valley.

Once Hanief was satisfied that it was all clear, Umar, Shams and ARQ came out one by one from under the bridge and hurriedly entered the cavity inside the truck. Manzoor told them that there were sufficient blankets, a small torch and packed food inside. After they were all in the truck, Manzoor bolted the door from outside and climbed into the driver's seat. He put his favourite Kashmiri music on and began to drive towards Udhampur along the national highway.

The sub-team, Naresh and Farha, heard every word spoken by Manzoor and Hanief. Once the truck had moved on, they followed it at a safe distance in an ambulance. Nek Mohammed, the police commando, was pretending to be the patient, lying on a stretcher with a drip attached to his wrist. They did not put on the siren deliberately, so the truck would continue to remain in front. The national highway had its usual amount of fast-paced traffic, and it was easy for them to avoid being noticed.

The truck reached the Sarore toll plaza, where Manzoor paid the toll and moved on. They then approached the Kunjwani police checkpoint, where the truck had to slow down to navigate the steel barriers. Manzoor held his breath, hoping that they would not be stopped. There was one policeman and his buddy there, who gave the truck a cursory look and allowed it to pass. It was now 4.30 a.m. Manzoor drove on the Jammu bypass and reached Sidhra, where the policeman at the naka signalled him to stop. Manzoor took out a Rs 500 note and slipped it into the hands of the constable who had stopped him. Without exchanging any more words, Manzoor drove away. The naka head constable kept quiet.

As they moved ahead, Shams realized he wanted to ease himself and knocked at the glass partition behind the back of Manzoor's seat. Manzoor could sense the knocking on the glass partition and indicated that it was not safe to stop the truck at that moment.

Back in the ambulance, Naresh and Farha tried to listen to the conversation, but the music inside the truck was loud and drowned out anything that was being said. It was time to put in place 'Plan B'. A Quick Reaction Team, in a bullet-resistant vehicle, was positioned to reach them within five minutes in case the truck stopped before Nagrota. They sent out the signal, and the well-equipped vehicle, manned by Zaheer and his team, began moving towards Sidhra. They were in an improvised bullet-resistant 407 mini troop carrier, which from the outside looked like a civilian vehicle. When they reached the Jagti crossing, the ambulance that was ahead put on the right indicator. It was a signal that all was well and they could move ahead without intervening.

* * *

Manzoor Trali soon reached the checkpoint near Nagrota, where he was told to pull over the vehicle to the side of the road. Rajveer and his team were watching every movement from the bullet-resistant command vehicle parked at a distance. It had powerful hydraulic high-mast PTZ cameras so the feed could be seen inside the cabin; a place on top to mount light machine guns; an announcement system to address people; and an emergency lighting system that could illuminate an area of at least 50 metres all around.

Manzoor kept calm. He was confident that a cursory look at the vehicle would not raise any suspicion. Even if someone climbed to the top of the truck, it would not be possible to detect the cavity. Manzoor was asked to show the vehicle's documents while the QRT commander at the location brought in the bulletproof vehicle to the left of the truck and parked it close to its side gate. Police commandos immediately got down and took positions behind sandbag bunkers covering all possible escape routes. Rajveer passed instructions to both cut-off teams placed a kilometre away on either side to stop vehicular traffic to avoid collateral damage. ASI Ram Kumar hurriedly asked the toll plaza employees to get inside one room.

As soon as Manzoor saw police commandos taking their positions, he knew that there was going to be trouble. He remained calm and asked for permission to go back inside the truck to get more documents. The naka team allowed it. As soon as he entered the cabin, he took out his pistol hidden under his seat and began firing at the naka party. Sub-inspector Rafeeq Ahmed was injured and his buddy fired back, hitting Manzoor. Hearing shots being fired, ARQ and his team quickly moved around some rice bags and blocked the left side of the cavity which was near the side door. They then entrenched themselves. Slowly they removed the upper cover of the cavity and the tarpaulin covering them and took positions with their M-4 rifles and grenades. They had sufficient stock of weapons and ammunition with them.

Shams hurled a grenade from the top of the truck and then jumped out from the back and ran towards the ravines on the left. The grenade exploded on the road close to the bullet-resistant vehicle. Shams was immediately shot down by the team covering the escape route there. The terrorists inside the truck began shooting, and the QRT team retaliated with heavy fire into the truck. Bullets flew all over but not a single one hit the remaining three terrorists since the rice bags provided them good cover.

Rajveer now took command and asked his men to hold fire. He used the announcement system to address everyone from inside the command vehicle. He told the second QRT to throw chilli grenades inside the truck. This was done immediately, but the grenades—non-lethal and made from bhut jolokia—exploded on top of the truck and did not affect the terrorists inside the cavity. Sensing that the effort had not achieved the desired result, a tear gas grenade was then thrown in, while everyone continued to hold fire. This exploded close to the cavity, and the terrorists started coughing. The teams could now figure out where the other terrorists were hiding. As they coughed, the terrorists kept firing upwards intermittently, in case anyone tried to enter the truck from the top.

It was now daylight. Rajveer took the microphone again and ordered the terrorists to surrender.

In response, ARQ shouted from inside, 'You are all kafirs!'

Repeated orders to surrender had no effect on the terrorists and they continued to fire and lobby grenades at the police team. A small drone with a camera was now flown over and around the truck to figure out the condition of the terrorists inside since much of the tarpaulin was burnt by this time. They could clearly see that Manzoor was dead inside the front cabin. Inside the cavity, three terrorists were still holed up, out of whom one was injured. Rajveer could see each and everything inside the command room, where he had the drone controller. At this time, the terrorists fired at the drone and shot it down, and Rajveer lost the footage. Another drone was flown in, a bigger one with a tear-gas attachment. It flew over the truck and dropped the shell inside the cavity. The terrorists were completely blinded now, and taking this opportunity, an attempt was now made to approach the cavity from the front of the truck. Police commando Zahir Ali quickly climbed on the front bonnet and then to the top of the front cabin and waited till the tear smoke effect was gone. He had a wet handkerchief on his face to avoid being blinded by the tear gas. However, he couldn't help coughing, thereby revealing his position. The terrorists, although blinded, hurled a grenade outside the cavity, which exploded five feet away from Zahir Ali. He escaped with minor injuries since he was lying completely flat behind rice bags. Rajveer radioed him to fall back immediately.

It was now time to use their full firepower against the terrorists. A multi-grenade launcher was pressed into service. Multiple grenades pierced through the rice bags and exploded. Within ten minutes, the terrorists were exposed completely. ARQ and Hanief, though sensing that they had no scope of escaping, made one last attempt and tried to jump out while firing indiscriminately. Alert police commandos brought both of them down. Umar, who was already injured, could not come out and was shot dead.

The operation was over.

Rajveer asked for one last sortie of the drone to check for any survivors. Once it was clear that all the terrorists were dead, the fire tender was brought in to douse the fire. Immediately after, police commandos went inside the truck following the room-intervention technique and cleared the site—a commando with a bullet-resistant shield moved in front, the others taking cover behind him. Then two commandos would move to two corners and do a speculative fire. In case there was no response, they would move ahead following the same drill. All the AK-47 rifles, M-4 rifles and the remaining grenades and ammunition were recovered. The GPS device was also seized in a partially broken condition and immediately sent to the lab for examination.

While searching the bags, Rajveer came across ARQ's mini torch, which had his name inscribed on it. He was stunned when he realized that one of the men had been Abdul Rehman Qadri—one of the most wanted terrorists in India. He quietly slipped the torch into his pocket as a souvenir of the biggest terrorist he had defeated.

Chapter 20

It was time for the police to celebrate their massive victory. Rajveer went to the police headquarters where the director general of police hugged him and congratulated his team. He immediately called up the Governor and then the Union security adviser and apprised them of the huge success. The Union interior minister himself came on the call and congratulated Rajveer. A dinner was thrown by the director general for the entire team, where they were handsomely rewarded. The injured were recommended for a Shaurya Chakra and Police Medal for Gallantry.

The recovered GPS device led the team to the tunnel that had been constructed for the terrorists. The border guards recovered evidence of the Pakistani hand in the attempted attack, including the sandbags from Karachi, Pepsi bottles made in Pakistan and a couple of empty oxygen cylinders that Haseeb had not taken back with him. This evidence would be used as further proof of Pakistani involvement in terror activities in India.

* * *

On the other side of the Pir Panjal range, in the Kashmir Valley, another of Rajveer's teams struck at an arms dump belonging to Chaudhary Alam in a remote village in Kupwara district. Their source led them to three 2000-litre capacity syntax tanks buried in the ground in an isolated area near the forest. The recoveries included fifty AK-47 rifles, machine guns, ammunition in plenty, grenades carefully packed in separate bags, night-vision devices, RDX to make explosives, circuits and timer devices, letter pads belonging to the Lashkar-e-Jabbar, mobile phones and SOS medicines. Chaudhary Alam was arrested for arms smuggling.

A second team in the Kashmir Valley raided the residential premises of Manzoor Trali and recovered documents regarding the activities of the Al Shafa Trust. Based on evidence regarding its activities, Asifa, Manzoor Trali's wife, was arrested on charges of terror funding. On the basis of disclosures made by Asifa, Zafarullah, the accountant working for the Lashkar-e-Jabbar, was also arrested.

The Lashkar-e-Jabbar in India was now badly hit. Their top commander in Kashmir, Manzoor Trali, had been eliminated, their arms supplier, Chaudhary Alam, was behind bars, and their stock of arms and ammunition had been seized.

* * *

It was dejection all over in the Lashkar-e-Jabbar camp at Bahawalpur. Curse of the pir! Maulana Asgar and Maulana Zaif were completely distraught and in mourning.

They had lost their biggest asset, ARQ, and the longest-surviving and most trusted associate, Manzoor Trali. Such was the magnitude of the loss that Maulana Zaif sent out a fifty-two-page obituary, named '*Allah ka Zabardast Banda*' (Awesome one chosen by Allah), dedicated to Manzoor Trali. Apart from these losses, the Al Shafa Trust had been exposed—their terror financing network which had worked for almost two decades was completely disrupted. The Lashkar-e-Jabbar decided to wind up active operations; they would wait for the Taliban regime to resume in Afghanistan to help them revive and receive a new set of mujahideen to restart their objective of separating Kashmir from India.

Chapter 21

A restless Maulana Zaif couldn't sleep that night. The failure of the operation was difficult to digest and his thoughts kept him twisting and turning in bed. He went through all kinds of emotions and fell into a syndrome called Gambling Disorder in psychiatry. Like a gambler who, despite losing at every try, thinks that victory lies in the next game, Maulana Zaif desperately wanted to make one last attempt.

It is said that when no one comes to your help, there is God. For the Lashkar-e-Jabbar, Sameer—aka 'Doctor'—was no less than God.

Doctor was the grand old man of the Lashkar-e-Jabbar. He had a very successful Ayurvedic medicine business. He had lost one brother to jihad, and the other was in Spain, running a garment business. Their mother had settled with him in Spain. His sister was married to the local Toyota showroom owner. Doctor did not need the help of the mujahideen to sustain himself, although his pension would

have been high for what he had done for them for the past
twenty years.

Although Doctor had retired from active involvement
in Lashkar-e-Jabbar activities, he considered it his duty to
reach out to Maulana Zaif and pay his condolences for the
death of the mujahideen.

Maulana Asgar and Zaif were sitting on the Iranian
carpet laid out in the meeting hall at the Lashkar-e-Jabbar
headquarters at Bahawalpur as visitors poured in to pay
their condolences. The family members of the fidayeen
sat beside the maulanas. Doctor waited in one corner of
the room, observing everyone there. The visitors included
ISI men, serving brigadiers of the army, residents of the
mohalla around and mujahideen commanders of all the
organizations who had their headquarters nearby.

Maulana Asgar spotted Doctor sitting in a corner and
understood that Doctor wanted to meet him privately.

After the visitors in the room had left, Maulana
signalled Saleem not to allow any more people in and
then asked Doctor to follow him to his personal chamber.
Maulana Zaif came too.

In the chamber was a huge picture of Kabah, a
Kashmiri samovar on one side of the room, a mat, cushions
and pillows on the carpet, and a silk-on-silk prayer mat for
offering namaz. It was sunset and all three prepared for the
Maghrib namaz.

After the namaz was over, Maulana Asgar asked for tea
to be served and then started talking. While Maulana Asgar
had founded the Lashkar-e-Jabbar, Doctor had been in this
business for longer than him. He was senior to him in the

erstwhile Harkat-ul-Mujahideen. Doctor had himself gone through various ups and downs, losing one of his brothers in Kashmir while working for the mujahideen. He had lost one leg himself while attempting to infiltrate the second time, when he stepped on a landmine at the border. It happened right on the Line of Control at Rajouri, after which his associates had pulled him over to the other side. The Pakistani rangers had been quick to raise the white flag after the sound of explosion, in order to save Doctor from being killed.

After Doctor had paid his condolences for the death of ARQ and his team, Maulana Zaif explained his plan to stall active operations in Kashmir for some time till they regrouped and had enough numbers in their fold. It would take at least six months to train a fresh batch of mujahideen, and in the meanwhile, they would also develop another set of contacts in Kashmir to give them the much-needed overground support.

'Do we have some mujahideen left in the Valley?' asked Doctor.

'Yes we do,' replied Maulana Zaif. 'But we don't have the finances and support needed to do anything in the Valley right now.'

'Leave that to me,' said Doctor.

During his first stint in the Kashmir Valley, Doctor had developed enough contacts there. There were many he could rely on completely for any kind of work.

'This is not the time to completely shut operations,' said Doctor. 'We should give a befitting reply to the security forces in Jammu and Kashmir. Operations can then be halted for some time till we regroup and recoup.'

Maulana Zaif's eyes lit up. He had spent the whole night thinking of ways to have one more go in Jammu and Kashmir. Doctor gave him hope.

Doctor tasked the Lashkar-e-Jabbar office with looking for returnees to Jammu and Kashmir who were visiting Pakistan on a valid visa. They reported back that three relatives of residents of Bahawalpur were returning to Jammu the next week. Doctor bought a steel tiffin carrier with a thermal outer case from the local market, carefully removed the mid-layer and packed in Indian 2000-rupee notes to make it one lakh of rupees. He then sealed it to appear like a normal tiffin and asked the Lashkar-e-Jabbar HQ to pack food and give it to Chacha Zafar, who was returning home after two months of stay at Bahawalpur. After reaching his home in Doda, he would have to hand over the empty tiffin to Shakeel Sheikh, who was a hardcore supporter of Jamaat-e-Islami and a staunch supporter of Doctor. Chacha Zafar did not realize that he was carrying cash for a Lashkar-e-Jabbar overground worker.

One of the 2000-rupee notes had an Echochat ID and password, which Shakeel Sheikh used to open an Echochat account. There was another virtual number written on another note, which he had to contact after opening his Echochat account. Shakeel sent a test message to Doctor on the number and immediately got a reply: AA bhai—*As salaam alaikum bhai*.

Doctor then made a call to Shakeel and asked him to arrange logistics at Jammu. He asked him to purchase a second-hand motorcycle in running condition for the mujahideen to use when needed. He also instructed him to take a room on rent in Qasim Nagar, on the outskirts of

Jammu city, which had a predominantly migrant Muslim population.

Shakeel set out towards Jammu the next day and started looking for a house to rent. He spoke to a few landlords, but they refused to give their house on rent to a single man. Tired after the house-hunting, he walked to a nearby restaurant and ordered a paratha. The waiter, Shabbir, while serving him, asked, 'Are you new around here?'

'Yes. I'm searching for a home for my kids,' replied Shakeel.

The two got talking and soon realized that they were from nearby villages in Doda: Shabbir was from Ghat, and Shakeel was from Bharat.

This created a bond, and Shabbir said he could get his friend's house on rent for Shakeel. His friend, Iqbal, worked in a local walnut factory and usually stayed there. He was unmarried and had a small but functional house in Qasim Nagar. Shabbir said he knew him well and that he would negotiate a reasonable rent for Shakeel.

They both went to the walnut factory and took the keys from Iqbal. At the house, Shakeel scanned the building and the area from the perspective of the mujahideen. It was on the outskirts of Jammu city and was surrounded by houses with terraces that were so close, they almost connected. Raika forest was nearby and offered a good escape route in case of an emergency. The route to the house was a narrow, winding lane. Everything about the house looked perfect for the mujahideen.

Shakeel went back to Iqbal and finalized the house at a monthly rent of Rs 15,000 for an initial period of six months. He paid the advance for three months out of the money Doctor had sent him. He now had to buy a second-hand motorcycle. Shabbir offered to help him out with this too. He contacted a local second-hand vehicle dealer and fixed up a 2010 model Hero Honda motorcycle for Rs 30,000, but told Shakeel that it would cost him Rs 40,000.

To his surprise, Shakeel agreed without bargaining. Shakeel knew that money was not a problem for the Lashkar-e-Jabbar. Shabbir was happy with the quick Rs 10,000 he'd made.

That night, Shakeel stayed at the newly rented house. He found a restaurant nearby, whose waiter Rameez agreed to deliver food to him 24/7. He ordered naan and kheema mutter for the night, ate and then went to sleep.

Doctor then turned to his old trusted aide, the chief of Harkat-ul-Jihad-e-Islami 313 Brigade (HUJI 313), to arrange for two fidayeen in Jammu. The holy month of Ramzan was to start on 4 July. The seventeenth day is the most significant one in the month of Ramzan; it is when the holy prophet went to the heavens in his physical self. It is also said that, on this day, at the end of a fierce battle, the faithful army (313 in number) gained victory through the help of Allah over a large army. This, Doctor decided, would be the day when they would attack. Doctor looked for a suitable target and learnt that the Union security adviser would be in Jammu on the seventeenth day of Ramzan, 21 July, to attend an event on 22 July.

Doctor felt as if Allah was guiding him in this holy mission: everything seemed to be falling in place so easily.

Amir Kashmiri was the chief of the HUJI 313 Brigade and had very few aides available in the Kashmir Valley.

He was also old by this time, and the dwindling financial support of the ISI made him even weaker. He had almost wound up operations in Kashmir and was looking for ways to pull out the remaining two Pakistani mujahideen, who had by now spent more than five years in the Kashmir Valley. Now, Amir asked them for one last favour. He promised them a safe exit after they achieved their final mission.

Abu Jindal and Abu Osama agreed. They were told that an associate would shift them to Jammu in a taxi without weapons. The required weapons would be sent through drones, which would be collected by another set of people completely unknown to the first one.

Doctor now took command, sitting at the Bahawalpur headquarters of the Lashkar-e-Jabbar. Amir Kashmiri was invited as a special guest and was given a room next to Maulana Asgar in the VVIP suite meant for the chiefs of any group that visited Bahawalpur. He intended to stay there till the operation was over.

Doctor coordinated with all the modules. An old contact from Kulgam, code name Akbar, was given the job of collecting weapons after a drone drop at a given GPS location at Deig rivulet near Samba. He would pick up the weapons and conceal them in two bags meant for the two fidayeens, and then leave them at a given GPS location at Qasim Nagar on 20 July. Shakeel was given the same GPS location and time and asked to wait till a vehicle dropped the two bags at 1 a.m. Shakeel had to simply pick up the bags and go home without asking any questions.

Someone with the code name Jehangir was tasked to pick up Abu Jindal and Abu Osama from their hideout in a dense jungle above Shopian, and then travel in a van full of empty vegetable crates. Both were given a fake UID card for identification in case they were asked for it at a checkpost. Jehangir was also given a GPS location at Qasim Nagar, but it was a different place from where Shakeel had to receive Abu Jindal and Abu Osama following the same procedure. Care was taken to ensure that nothing between the two modules was common except Shakeel, who did not know anything more than that they were both sent by Doctor and some big task was being planned, which Doctor would reveal at the last moment.

Doctor was taking care to ensure that none of the mistakes committed previously by the Lashkar-e-Jabbar were repeated.

The evening of 20 July was hectic for Shakeel. He had to first receive the two fidayeens at 10.30 p.m., drop them at his house and then head to another location at 1 a.m. to pick up two bags.

Akbar moved out of Shopian at 4 p.m. and took the route through Kulgam to hit the national highway near the newly opened Navyug tunnel. He then moved towards Udhampur where the vehicle was asked to stop at the Jakhaini police naka. The policemen at the naka looked around and, seeing the empty vegetable crates loaded in the Tata 207 vehicle, asked Akbar to proceed. Akbar then drove to Jammu. The highway bypass led him straight to Qasim Nagar colony where he took a left turn and entered the colony. From there he fed in the given GPS location on Google Maps and followed the instructions. It led him to mohalla Narwal Bala, from where he turned into a narrow lane. Had it been daytime, he would have been stuck in a traffic jam.

Akbar reached the given GPS location at around
10.45 p.m. and found a masked man waiting. He put on
the right signal indicator as instructed by Doctor, although
there was no right turn there. Seeing the signal, Shakeel
approached the driver and asked, '*Ghode aaye hain?*'

Akbar got down and removed a few empty vegetable
crates. Two men appeared, got down from the vehicle
and started walking with Shakeel. Akbar drove away
immediately, proceeding back towards the Kashmir Valley.

Shakeel took the men to his rented house and asked
them if they wanted food. Communication was done
through gestures because they spoke in a language that was
different from the local Dogri. Shakeel figured that they
might be from Afghanistan. He had heard mujahideen
from Afghanistan speak Pashto, and when the two men
spoke to each other, the language sounded familiar. The
men conveyed that they were hungry. They were fasting
during the month of Ramzan and had had only dates after
last light to break the fast while they were driving towards
Jammu. After a heavy meal of mutton biryani, they changed
and went to sleep.

Shakeel waited for another two hours and then
went out to receive the two bags. Such confidence did
Doctor have in Shakeel that he hadn't even told him
what would be in the bags. Shakeel had simply been told
to hand over the bags to the two fidayeens. After walking
for about five minutes, Shakeel reached the location and
waited. A Tata Sumo arrived at 1.05 a.m. and the man
inside handed over the bags to Shakeel and drove away.
Shakeel put both bags on his shoulders. They were heavy,
and he could feel the pinch of the nozzle of a weapon.

An experienced hand, Shakeel could make out that the bags had at least an AK-47 rifle each. The clatter of magazines could also be heard while he walked. He took a little longer than five minutes to reach the house, having to stop twice to take a breath and to ease the weight on his shoulders.

When he reached home, he found the two visitors still sleeping. He put the bags to one side and went to bed as well. He set an alarm for 4 a.m., the time for the Fajr namaz and for food before fasting started.

Early the next morning, after he and the visitors had woken up, they did the wudu and prepared for the namaz. He took out his mobile and spoke to Doctor on Dialog.

'Everything is fine here,' he said. '*Ghoda aur pithoo, dono pahunch gaye hain* [The horse and the bags have both reached].'

Shakeel was so used to speaking in coded language that, despite knowing that Dialog was impossible to intercept, it was the way he still communicated with Doctor. Doctor was equally comfortable with this and understood what Shakeel meant.

'Tonight, you have to take them near the site of the function. Drive your Santro car ahead and the mujahideen will follow on their motorcycle. When you reach the naka, keep the parking light on. They will understand that they have to attack at that place. You then move ahead and the mujahideen will do their work,' Doctor said. He explained in detail each minute precaution to be taken to ensure their safety. Doctor also wanted an exit route in case the squad was able to get out without being hurt. He asked Shakeel to wait at a distance of a kilometre ahead of the naka. Care was taken to keep him at a sufficient distance so that Shakeel himself did not get trapped in the firing.

Doctor planned to hit the naka closest to the venue of the visit of the Union security adviser to send a message that they could attack one of the most protected people of India.

Shakeel then made the mujahideen talk to Doctor, and they spoke to him in Pashto. After they hung up the phone, having understood the instructions, Shakeel offered them food but they refused, citing roza. The plan was to leave just after having food after the Fajr namaz so that they had all the required energy to survive a long-drawn battle.

At 5 p.m., Shakeel received a call from his daughter, who was nine years old. She asked him where he was and told him that she was missing him a lot. He spoke to her for a few minutes and tried to hang up the phone, but his daughter insisted on speaking for longer. She made him promise that they would go to Doodh Pathri for a picnic and Shakeel agreed.

After hanging up, Shakeel thought about his next move. He loved his children and it was after persistent efforts that he had managed to get his name out of the overground workers list with the Kashmir police. He was now free to move and had a decent business selling fruits to sustain himself and his family. His daughter, Safeena, had got admission to the Presentation Convent through a contact in the HRD ministry in Jammu and Kashmir. He wanted to give the best education to his children so they could get away from the struggle in Kashmir.

Shakeel was developing cold feet. There was now little time left for them to leave for the attack site. He decided to make an excuse. When it was time to leave, he held his stomach and pretended to cry in pain. Both the fidayeens went to him and asked if he was all right. They then made a WhatsApp video call to Doctor. Doctor was angry, but kept his cool. He said he would arrange another contact who could reach them within the hour.

Doctor got in touch with Farooq, who belonged to Pulwama and had settled as a fruit vendor in the same mohalla at Qasim Nagar. He agreed to do whatever Doctor asked him. He was a loyalist who had served alongside Doctor during his tenure in the Kashmir Valley. Settling his close contacts in Jammu and sustaining them for so long was a part of Doctor's long-term vision, and it was paying off.

Doctor asked Farooq not to take his mobile but to use an old SIM card from the stock that was unused so far. Farooq put a SIM into a new Android mobile phone, rushed to the local mobile recharge shop and asked for a recharge of Rs 399.

* * *

In the electronic surveillance unit of the Crime Branch in Jammu, there was a flash on the computer screen.

A long time back, Rajveer had infiltrated some SIM cards into the Lashkar-e-Jabbar set-up, expecting dividends in due course. Like Doctor, Rajveer also had a long-term vision and plans that would eventually yield results.

'Sir, one of our SIMs sent to the Lashkar-e-Jabbar in 2018 has just been activated,' said Rohit, who was manning the ESU.

'Find the location of the SIM immediately and keep it on live tracking,' said Rajveer.

After a minute, Rohit said, 'The SIM is located in Qasim Nagar in Jammu.'

Rajveer asked for a quick meeting and briefing at the SOG headquarters at Jammu and a Quick Reaction Team immediately headed towards Qasim Nagar in two civilian vehicles. The QRT members were in plain clothes and were well-armed. They were briefed to follow the holder of the SIM card. The live location of Farooq was diverted to the mobile of Manohar, the in-charge of the QRT.

It was 9 p.m. by now.

The QRT deboarded their vehicles a kilometre away from Farooq's location. They split into two groups and headed towards two different lanes leading to where Farooq was. After 9 p.m., during roza, movement on the road was limited, especially in a neighbourhood where the population was predominantly Muslim. The QRT ensured that they maintained a sufficient gap between themselves to avoid being noticed.

Manohar was the first person to sight Farooq heading towards a thick cluster of houses—he had the live location, and there was no one else moving on the road. He followed Farooq as stealthily as he could, indicating the other members of his team to follow. Rajiv, moving in the other lane, was asked to stop and wait and cover the exit route from the other side.

* * *

Farooq fed Doctor's number into his new mobile and called him on Echochat. He was immediately given the GPS location of where he had to reach. Doctor explained the task and said he had to drive a car ahead of the mujahideen and they would follow him on their motorcycle.

Farooq walked on the main road for a kilometre. He then turned on to a quiet lane and climbed up a gradual slope to reach the T-junction. From there, he took a left and reached the given GPS location. There was no one to receive him. He contacted Doctor, who asked him to send his live location on WhatsApp. Doctor then guided him. 'Take a left turn from there, then right after 50 metres and wait,' he said.

Farooq followed the instructions. He waited at the final location for five minutes and then got impatient. He called Doctor again, who asked him to send a small 360-degree video clip. Farooq did so. Certain that no one was following Farooq, Doctor asked Shakeel to come out of his house and hand over the keys to his car to the man there.

Manohar watched from a distance. It was not clear as to what exactly was happening. He moved in a bit closer and was now around 50 metres away, taking care that he was not visible.

Meanwhile, Shakeel came out of the house and went up to Farooq. He handed over the key to his car, but there were no signs of the fidayeens who had to follow on a motorcycle. Shakeel walked ahead and asked Farooq to follow. Seeing someone coming towards him, Manohar quickly moved into a bylane and pressed his body to the wall. Shakeel walked some distance looking left and right and observed someone standing along the wall in a lane on the right. It was extremely unusual at this time of night. He immediately ran back, indicating to Farooq that he should escape.

Farooq drove the car away at full speed. Manohar asked his rear party to block the vehicle, but he was going too fast for anyone to intervene. Shakeel went back into the by-lane, reached the house and raised an alarm. The mujahideen picked up their backpacks, filled their magazines and put the spare ammunition in their bags. They then took out their suicide vests especially sent by Doctor for the attack and wore them carefully, ensuring that the switch did not get activated. It was meant to be exploded in the crowded junction where people would gather to get frisked before getting inside the main venue. Grenades were packed inside the four pockets on the camouflage jacket, which they wore over the suicide vest. They took Shakeel's mobile phone and asked him to flee.

* * *

When Manohar saw Shakeel run away after spotting him, he alerted his men. It was clear that there were terrorists around. They had been getting intelligence inputs that terrorists may try to disrupt the visit of the Union security adviser, and this confirmed it for him. He asked for additional reinforcements and immediately got his QRT to block the exit routes to the target mohalla. They didn't know the exact house where they might be hiding. It was 11 p.m. by now and they had no option but to wait for the first light to start searching the mohalla for the terrorists. The Union Reserve Police Force (URPF) was deployed to surround the mohalla.

While they were taking their positions, the two fidayeens passed by in their camouflage uniform. Walking by a URPF party, they said 'Jai Hind'. The URPF man, little realizing that they could be terrorists, replied 'Jai Hind'. The two fidayeens moved out of the inner cordon and walked on at an easy pace. In the absence of a local guide, the two

Afghani-speaking attackers followed the nallah, hoping to come out of the cordon and find a suitable place where they could open fire and kill as many as possible.

Rajveer had by this time responded to the call of Manohar and sent in more URPF personnel to strengthen the cordon. While Rajiv was helping out the inducted forces to form the outer cordon, he stood at the culvert, taking cover, well aware that there were terrorists around and that there was a high probability that they would come across each other. At the moment when the bus carrying additional forces was about to reach the culvert, Rajiv spotted some movement there. This was not where the deployment was supposed to be stationed. Suspicious, he immediately shouted and signalled for the driver to stop. As soon as the driver slowed down, the terrorists emerged from under the culvert and fired at the bus. The troops were taken by surprise. Before they could retaliate, the attackers lobbed grenades and also fired with the under-barrel grenade launcher (UBGL). Eight personnel were injured, two of them critically. Rajiv came out from cover and immediately took on the terrorists from behind. They were taken by surprise, not expecting retaliation from that direction. One of them turned back and fired a volley of rounds at Rajiv and his team. He received bullet injuries in his thigh and in the abdomen and fell down. His PSOs were also injured. Before the bleeding could completely drain Rajiv, he mustered whatever strength he had and fired back from where he was lying on the ground. Both terrorists were injured and ran back towards a house—belonging to a Rashid Gujjar—and took shelter in the toilet there.

Hearing the sound of gunfire, Manohar ran back and entered his Rakshak vehicle, a bulletproof troop carrier meant to keep its men secure. He then quickly reversed it and moved towards the culvert. He saw Rajiv lying on the road and his PSOs crawling towards the shops on the side of the road. Manohar immediately called for more bulletproof vehicles, and then picked up Rajiv and his PSOs with the help of his escort personnel and put them inside the Rakshak. Iqbal, the paramedic with the team, immediately put all the injured on drips and gave them SOS injections. Rajiv was fast losing blood and had, by this time, become unconscious. Iqbal told Manohar that they needed to hurry to the hospital.

By now, Rajveer had arrived with reinforcements and immediately took charge. Manohar briefed him quickly and gave him an approximate indication of the location where the terrorists could be hiding. Rajveer asked Manohar to proceed to the hospital and also arranged another Rakshak for the other injured URPF personnel to be shifted.

Rajveer tightened the cordon and waited, talking continuously to Manohar who was on the way to the hospital. Manohar was sitting on the floor of the Rakshak with Rajiv's head in his lap. Rajiv was by now gasping and breathing heavily. Iqbal gave him another SOS injection, felt his pulse and counted. 55, 50, 45, 40 … His pulse rate was going down constantly.

'What's Rajiv's condition?' asked Rajveer.

Manohar looked at Iqbal, who indicated that it was almost over for Rajiv. He didn't have the courage to tell Rajveer. Iqbal took the phone from Manohar and informed Rajveer that there was no pulse.

Rajveer was shattered. He had lost one of his daredevil colleagues. Rajiv had been a part of many critical operations earlier and was a recipient of five gallantry medals, including the prestigious Shaurya Chakra. He flaunted his operational strength and posted pictures on social media of some of his daring operations, which were much liked by his friends. Rajveer put his head down, closed his eyes and prayed. He then regained his composure and took command.

At first light, they resumed the search. At this time, Rashid Gujjar's son went out to answer the call of nature. As soon as he reached the washroom outside, he saw a body lying near the door with a gun in hand, and another man standing there. He immediately ran back, shouting. The troops were alerted and called Rashid's son for questioning. He said that there were two men, of which one was most likely dead and the other was alive.

Rajveer took his men to the top of the roof of the adjacent house, from where he had a clear sight of the entrance of the toilet where the terrorists were hiding. He ordered his men to use the multi-grenade launcher to target the single brick wall of the toilet. It was not long before both the terrorists were killed.

Rajveer then called for the bomb disposal squad to clear the area and move the dead bodies. Many times in the past, suicide attackers removed the pin of a grenade and put it under their body before dying. Any careless handling of the dead body could lead to casualties in the security forces. The bomb disposal squad carefully took the bodies out, removed the suicide vests and exploded them in a controlled manner. He then entrusted the last formalities to his second-in-command and left for the hospital.

When he saw the dead body of Rajiv, he put his hands to his head. Tears rolled down his eyes. He then wiped away his tears and said to Manohar. 'Give him full honours. He was a braveheart and finished his work as usual before we arrived.'

Later that day, they held a wreath-laying ceremony at the Police Lines at Jammu. People lined up along the street to bid Rajiv farewell. The Union security adviser's visit went off without a hitch, and he visited Rajiv's family to pay his condolences.

The Lashkar-e-Jabbar had once again been vanquished. Even Doctor had not been able to give the Lashkar-e-Jabbar their much-needed success. This was the final nail in the coffin for them.

***

Nikita and the children visited Rajveer and his parents later that month. The mood was light as they enjoyed the success of his hard work and dedication.

As the family relaxed in the living room, Rajveer looked around and said a silent thank you that they were all safe and well.

It could well have been a scene straight out of a Bollywood movie. Nikita was talking to Aakriti and telling her she was old enough to start keeping her room and the house clean, and soon she would be ready for marriage. Rajveer smiled, thinking back to some twenty years ago, and silently withdrew from the room. Somewhere at the back of his mind, he knew it was not over yet. There was still a lot of work to be done, a lot more terrorists to be dealt with and many more ill-intended plans to be foiled so that his innocent countrymen could sleep well, knowing that their families were safe. He could feel the warmth in his heart as it swelled with pride and love for his country. He sighed, thinking, there was more to come ... The maliciously intentioned did not stop at anything ... but he knew that only the well-intentioned always won the battle, because there was always the curse of the pir!

Acknowledgements

This book would not have been possible without the undivided support of our families, who have been extremely patient and caring while we borrowed the time which was due to them to write this book. Our gratitude to each one of them.

We are very grateful to Deepthi Talwar, the editor, and Ralph Rebello, the copy editor, for their insightful critique and suggestions, some of which we have incorporated, and we beg their pardon for the ones that we could not accommodate, keeping our vision of the book in mind.

We are deeply indebted to all the officers and staff of J&K Police for putting their faith in the ability of their officers by giving them every opportunity to learn and grow while they serve the nation. The list would be incomplete without remembering all the officers and staff of J&K Police who have laid down their lives to protect their countrymen.

Last but definitely not least, we express our sincere thanks to our readers who have encouraged us by reading the book and give us reason to write more.